He Loves Me

I Wish Series, Volume 1

Beth Lauzier

Published by Seriously Awesome Books, 2020.

While every precaution has been taken in the preparation of this book, the publisher assumes no responsibility for errors or omissions, or for damages resulting from the use of the information contained herein.

HE LOVES ME

First edition. June 4, 2020.

Copyright © 2020 Beth Lauzier.

ISBN: 978-1734784206

Written by Beth Lauzier.

Also by Beth Lauzier

I Wish Series
He Loves Me

Watch for more at https://www.seriouslyawesomebooks.com.

To my grandma, Cora Wright. For always reading my first drafts and giving me your honest grandma opinion.

Chapter 1
Be careful what you wish for.

———

"And then I said, Mister President, you can't handle the truth." Kylie smacked a balled fist on the palm of her hand, emphasizing her point then jumped off the curb onto the street. Her bright green shoes splashed in a puddle sending water everywhere, soaking my feet.

"Wait; what?" Pausing a moment, I thought back on the conversation, but I was at a complete loss. Hopping off the curb, I followed behind her, trying to put together whatever I'd missed. My neon yellow flip-flops slapped the wet road as I rushed to catch up, but still, I was at a total loss.

"Hallelujah, she has returned." In an overly dramatic voice, Kylie shouted and strutted down the crosswalk like a runway model, fluffing her pink hair for the imaginary crowd. People stopped and stared, but once they saw it was just two teenagers, they ignored us. "Praise be she has returned from daydream land." Hopping onto the sidewalk, Kylie turned a one-eighty and struck a pose in her neon orange windbreaker, then added jazz hands for a more dramatic effect.

"Will you please stop?" Asking her to tone it down wouldn't do any good, but I tried anyway. Shifting my backpack higher, I hunched my shoulders and sighed. For what seemed like the tenth time today, I wished I was invisible. Kylie thrived in the public eye, but I preferred to get lost in the crowd.

"Hang on a sec." Tugging me to a stop, Kylie pulled out a sharpie and a pink piece of paper from her blue fluffy bag. She pushed my backpack aside, which caused it to fall and hit my leg. "So what was it this time, hmm. Come on, tell me. You and Garrett dancing in some giant ball-room like Beauty and the Beast?" Kylie hummed the theme song from the movie, and I rolled my eyes at her antics.

She placed the small paper square on my back, wrote down a number, then folded it into a paper crane. The bright little bird then went in a zip-lock bag and joined a dozen of its other multicolored bird friends. She stowed it all away in her bag, then linked arms with mine and pulled me down the street toward the school.

"What number are you on now?" Brushing some stray lock of red hair behind an ear, I grabbed Kylie's hand and tugged off her emergency hair tie, then pulled my hair up, giving my neck a little more airflow.

"One-eighty three." Kylie waved a hand wildly in a dismissive gesture. "I was right, though." She said in a sing-song voice. "You and Garrett sitting in a tree." Humming the rest of the song, Kylie did a weird dance as she walked alongside me. I whacked her with the back of my hand, but she started to sing louder, much to my flaming embarrassment.

Stopping suddenly, she picked a daisy, then spun around and dropped to a knee in front of me. "Paisley, will you do me the esteemed honor of going to the fall dance with me?" Kylie deepened her voice to sound like Garrett, but she did a very poor job at it. I couldn't help but laugh and play along with her antics, though.

"I'd thought you'd never ask. Of course, I'll accompany you." I took the flower, held it to my chest, and batted my eyelashes like an airhead, causing Kylie to rock with laughter.

She linked arms with me again, and we continued to school. "Why do you even like that guy? He's not nice or even interesting for that mat-ter."

I smacked her on the shoulder with the flower and skipped over a puddle. "It's rude to talk bad about people." She snorted at my comment but knew I was right and didn't argue farther. "He's funny and cute and..." Before I could add anything more, Kylie butted in with a short list of her own.

"And he's popular, the captain of the football team, and some would say good looking. Which he knows and uses to the full extent of look-dom." She made an angry gesture and huffed like the fact some people use how they look to get things offended her. Which okay, fair, but...

"Look-dom isn't a word." Not missing the next puddle, I stomped my flip-flop in the water, getting Kylie's shoes wet in the process. The cold water was shocking, but a wet foot was worth it.

She hissed at the rainwater now soaking her feet and glared at me. "I'm just saying you can do a whole lot better. Don't get stuck on a guy who's shallow as a puddle." Smiling gleefully, Kylie kicked some water at my feet and ran ahead with a high squeal to get out of backsplash range.

I watched her pink head bob through the small crowd of others heading to school and twirled the flower as I let what she said float around my brain. She was right, of course, but it would be nice to be noticed by him just once in my life. Going to all the football game after-parties and being popular. As shallow as it was, I'd still like to be a part of it all, if only for a short time.

Smelling the flower, I ran through that daydream again for a minute. I plucked one of the white flower petals as my mind floated around and felt the waxy surface briefly before letting it drift to the ground. "He loves me," I said to no one, then plucked another petal and let it float in the wind. "He loves me not."

I continued plucking the waxy white petals until only one was left. Picking the last one, I stopped and stared at it for a moment. "He loves me." With a sigh, I flung both the petal and stem aside, if only things could be that easy. But life didn't work that way. Love was messy and downright hard sometimes. You couldn't just make wishes on something and poof, your life was now perfect.

Rolling my eyes at the odd thought, I jogged the rest of the way to school and weaved my way through the people standing outside waiting for the bell to ring. Kylie hadn't made it into the building yet; she'd stopped and was chatting with Nancy by the main doors. Just by all the hand motions, I could tell what they were talking about. I adjusted my backpack, fortifying myself for the day ahead before wandering over.

"But then I was all; I am not kissing him. And Miss Armod agreed with me." Kylie huffed, resting both hands on her hips like she carried a large burden. "I'll tell ya, the life of an actor." With a roll of her eyes, Nancy bumped a shoulder into mine and smiled in greeting.

Grabbing some hair that had escaped her bun, Nancy pinned the black strands back in place and adjusted her glasses. Nancy rocked an overly large long sleeve shirt and holey jeans. Somehow she managed to not look like a hobo. "So, you going to the dance this year?" I inwardly groaned at both their smiles. It seemed everyone knew about my crush.

Before I could answer, the bell rang, and everyone started to head inside. "Uh, time to get to class." Nancy lifted an eyebrow and smirked at my quick topic change but didn't give me any grief as I linked arms them both and hurried us inside. All the while, Kylie regaled us with another story from drama class. The girl needed to be a writer for all the wild stories she had up her sleeve.

After getting elbowed in the side one too many times, I swerved and fought my way through the crowd of people in the small hallway. The noise seemed to bounce off the walls and made it ten times louder. But then again, it was always too loud first thing in the morning.

Grumbling under my breath about morning people, I found my locker and waved goodbye to Nancy as she walked against the flow of half-asleep people trying to get to class. I opened the combo lock, then ripped open a bag of red Jojo fish and ate one of the little gummy fishes.

"Those are so gross." I moved the locker door aside and gawked at Kylie before holding out the bag and offering her one of the most amazing candies ever. She made a gagging sound as she turned and pretended to upchuck. Scoffing at her antics, I watched her pull out some paper and make another bird. This one was light blue with little white flowers on it.

"These," I held up the bag of fish for her inspection, "are amazing. You just don't know what's good for you." Laughing at her pinched up face, I grabbed another fish and munched. I rolled the bag of gummies up and stuck them in my locker with books I wouldn't need until later in the day.

Someone tapped on my shoulder lightly, and I turned to see who it was, only to fall into the bluest eyes I'd ever seen staring down at me. So engrossed in his eyes, all the noise and chaos in the early morning hallway seemed to fade away. Until Kylie kicked the back of my shoes, nearly buckling my knee and making me kiss the locker.

I bit my lip and sent a glare her way, but darn her acting skills. Her face may have remained blank, but her eyes were laughing at me. "Talk to ya later, amiga." Kylie slammed her locker closed and skipped down the hall. People moved aside like the parting of the Red Sea. I had no clue how she did that, but she needed to teach me her ways.

Another tap on the shoulder and I slowly turned back to mister blues-eyes himself, Garrett Price. Captain of the football team, student body president, most popular guy in school, who wanted to talk to me.

Chapter 2

"So, what's your number?"

———

"So, I heard from the gossip tree you're the one to talk to about an English paper." It took a little longer than I'd like to admit to form a coherent thought in this jumbled up mess I called a brain.

"Uh...yeah." I winced at my lack of social grace and dug another book from my bag and stuck it in the locker just for the excuse not to look at him. Catching his profile from the corner of my eye, I checked out his abs, which were on display for all to see in his tight-fitting grey shirt.

Leaning a shoulder against the lockers, Garrett kept his gaze on me, and I felt unbalanced. A group of girls walked by and slowed down to take all of mister blue-eyes in, from the fitted shirt to his rich brown hair. They laughed and passed secrets behind their hands, and when Garrett caught them gawking, he smiled and winked at them. They giggled louder and rushed on to class in packs of three or more.

"I'd just like to brush up for tests coming up next week. Mister Cook is brutal with homework, and he's got it out for anyone on the ball team this year. Got to keep my grades up, or I can't play football. Ya know what I mean?" Garrett leaned a forearm on the lockers and crowded my space even more, seemingly taking all the air around us for himself. Seriously, your brain needs that stuff to work correctly, how can it do all the brain things with no air?

"Uh, yeah, totally." Another cringe at my lack of social skills. I ducked out from his invasion of personal space, then shut my locker with a bang.

"Great, we can get together and do something. Give me your phone." It took a second from lack of brain air to process his words. Finally, I fished my cell from a back pocket and handed it over. He started to type his number in, and I got the opportunity to study him closer without his eyes on me. Dark brown hair fell over his eyes, hiding them from view. I don't understand how guys could have messy hair and still look amazing. If I tried the same messy look, people would call for the troll hunters.

"Did ya catch the game last night?" Wyatt Moore slung an arm around Garrett's neck and locked him in a chokehold. "Someone owes me fifty bucks, man." He let up when he saw me and flashed a stunning smile my way. He tipped his grey fedora back and ran his gaze down the length of my body. "Well, well, who's this pretty thing?" Standing a little over six feet tall with broad shoulders and defined muscles, Wyatt was another guy Kylie would say knew he was good looking and used it to his advantage. Another tight shirt and snug jeans, Wyatt oozed charm with his attitude and hat. But those weren't what girls whispered about behind a cupped hand. It was the perfect smile and laughing eyes that at this moment were set full-force on me.

I covered my chest with a book and took a step back, wanting to recover some personal space. Wyatt was a player if I'd ever seen one. He had an amazing bronze skin tone from his mixed parents and never lacked attention from most girls in school. "Hey man, this is Peyton, she's going to help me with some school work." Garrett gave me a megawatt smile then shoved a hand in the pocket of his jeans.

"Nice to meet ya. Maybe I could get help with school work, too." Wyatt waggled his eyebrows, then took my hand and kissed it, trying to be charming, but it fell flat.

Pulling my hand back, I resisted the urge to wipe away the grossness. "Actually, the name's Paisley, and I don't have the time to help you." I gave him a once over trying to let him know I found him lacking when in actuality, he was anything but. This didn't seem to phase him one bit as he simply shrugged my comment off with a smile.

He pulled off his fedora, hugged it to his chest, and gave me a deep bow. "Seems the lady only has eyes for one." He ran a hand through his dark hair then punched Garrett on the shoulder. "Let me know how study time goes." He wagged his eyebrows at me again then strolled off, meeting up with more football players who were standing down the hall.

"Catch you later, man." Stepping into my space again, Garrett handed over my phone, and I stuck it in a back pocket just as the last bell rang. "See ya around, Paisley." Without another word, Garrett walked off and left me a little lightheaded.

I looked over my shoulder and watched him greet his friends from the team. Bro hugs and back slaps and a kiss on the cheek from Emily.

Emily Carter, head cheerleader and social queen of the school. Tall and blonde with a sun-kissed tan, Emily was always fashion-forward, and today was no exception. A bright pink, mid-sleeve shirt, and dark wash jeans. One wrong word from her and your social life was in the tank. I decide to move along and get to class before they noticed me.

But Garrett caught me staring and winked, leaving me in a stunned stupor. My face started to heat as butterflies tap-danced a jig in my gut. I may have started mentally planning our wedding at that moment. I shook my head, trying to clear the stupid thought from my oxygen-deprived brain. He'd just wanted some help with homework once maybe twice, then things would go back to normal.

But a little part of me wished it could turn into something more. Just once in my whole school lifetime, I'd like to be invited to the parties and dances. Go to the after football game parties and really be part of that crowd. But that's not the hand I had been dealt, and I should learn to live with it. Right?

Chapter 3

Cheese fries, chocolate shakes, and ranch don't mix.

———

I sat in Charlie's Diner and watched the rain fall instead of doing homework. The diner was a local hang out of sorts for most everyone in town. Good food at low prices and nice people. I probably ate here at least once a week with friends and saw most of the kids from school doing the same. Of course, being in a different social circle with the drama club and what Jeremy called the nerd herd of Willow Creek High, we didn't talk or even really acknowledge each other.

With a sigh, I dipped a cheese-covered fry in ranch dressing, took a bite, and got back to work. I had to finish before Kylie got here and distracted me with drama class drama. I mentally rolled my eyes at the thought of my overly dramatic friend and jotted down some more notes.

The bell over the door rang, but I ignored it until I heard his voice. A very wet football team waltzed through the door, shoving one another and loudly giving each other a hard time. And right behind them, the cheerleaders floated in looking perfect after practice, which I'm half convinced some kind of witchcraft had to be involved. In the back of my mind, I hated them a little for that. I looked like a drowned rat after any exercise and then add the downpour going on outside to that. With a shake of my head to clear the mean-spirited thoughts, I tried to tune out their loud joking and get more work finished.

So engrossed in my papers, I didn't notice Garrett until he slid into the booth and sat in front of me. "Hey." He ran a hand through wet hair, and I tracked a water drop as it trickled down his face to chin where it fell on the table, leaving a wet dot. "A bit wet out there, huh." He leaned in and folded both arms across the table like he had all the time in the world to chat.

The thought almost made me feel special until I heard his friends make kissy noises at us. I felt myself getting warm at the attention. Shifting my papers around, I pretended not to hear them, but Garrett simply turned and told them to stuff it. That didn't stop the glare from Emily, though.

"What ya studying?" Swiping a cheese fry from my plate, Garret gave his undivided attention to me as he ate. Annoyance prickled at the food swipe, and I seemingly didn't answer him fast enough. He slid a paper closer and took a moment to examine it. "Woah, is this what the test is going to be on?" I took the paper back before he got it wet and stacked it with all my other work away from prying eyes.

"No, I'm doing extra credit that way I can..." One of the waitresses, a girl I knew from math class, sauntered over with two shakes and set them on the table, a chocolate one with whipped cream and cherry in front of me and vanilla with the same topping in front of Garrett.

He gave her a wink, and she walked away, putting a little too much sway in her hips. She might dislocate something if she kept it up too long. Garrett watched her all the way back to the front counter. His eyes seemed glued to her backside. Wyatt let out a wolf whistle and fanned himself with his hat, not that the girl seemed to mind the attention from him.

"So extra credit, huh." Garrett's phone dinged, and his friends called him back over. But he waved them off and turned back to me.

"Yeah, I'm getting my masters in English, and I'll start some online classes in the next few weeks. Just wanted to get ahead so I won't stress over it as much." I plucked the cherry from my shake and popped the whole thing stem and all in my mouth.

He smiled and watched me with near unsettling attention. "That's cool, what are you studying for?" Garrett grabbed another one of my fries and dunked it in his shake. I shuddered at the thought of cheese and milkshake.

I put the cherry stem on my plate, a little knot in the middle of it now. "I want to be a librarian like my grandma." Thinking back to summers spent at the library and the way she could make books and stories so much fun, I chuckled and drank some of my shake, leaving me with a little chocolate mustache, which I wiped away quickly.

Garrett snorted and grabbed another fry. "You need a masters in English to tell kids to shush?" He popped the fry in his mouth, pulled out his phone, and started poking at it, missing the irritated look I shot him.

"Yeah, and being a librarian is more than telling people to be quiet." Angry at his belittling of what my grandmother did, I pulled out my phone and checked the time giving myself something to do other than talk to him.

Resting a hand on my arm, Garrett ducked and caught my eyes. "I didn't mean it. I'm sure being a librarian is great." A smile stretched across his face, and it showed off bright white teeth, but his voice clearly said being a librarian was lame. My chest ached a little at the dismissal. It may not be the most exciting job out there, but it was something I loved.

"Oh, am I interrupting something?" Emily leaned down and ran a hand down Garrett's arm until her breasts rested on his shoulder. If he turned, he'd get an eye full of what she's packing in that tight pink shirt.

"Nah, just talking junk. What you up too?" Garrett turned and got an eye full of Emily's padded bra of lies.

"I was getting lonely with no one to talk too." Pouting, she leaned in a little, practically falling into the booth in her attempt to get closer. "Come over and sit with us, you haven't forgotten about me, have you?" Turning the pout up to ten was such an air-head TV move, I couldn't hide an eye roll of longsuffering.

"How could I forget a face like yours?" I nearly gagged at the amount of cheese in the line. "I'll be there in a second." Garrett gave her a smile and chugged the rest of his shake. I shuttered at the thought of the brain freeze to come. "Text ya later." Sliding out of the booth with a hand on his head, Garret looked pained as Emily pulled him to the front where the rest of his friends were.

Before Emily sat, she turned back to me and put a possessive arm over Garrett's shoulders and smirked like she won whatever game we were playing. I ignored her and texted Jeremy while trying not to look over at the table full of loud, laughing people like an out of place loser.

Jeremy texted back quickly and let me know he'd be at school tomorrow. I hated his allergies were so bad this time of year, but at least he had a good attitude about it all.

"Okay, I'm here now, spill the beans chickie-poo." Kylie dropped her overly large fuzzy bag in the seat and sat in front of me, blocking the view of Garrett's table. "Why do you have a chocolate shake?" Digging through her messenger bag, she came up with a zip-lock baggie of square multi-colored paper and proceeded to dump everything claiming more than half the table for herself.

"Garrett bought it for me, but you can have it." I pushed the shake toward her, making a small path through her mess. The whipped cream was now melted and looked unappetizing, or at least to me. The same waitress from before strolled over with a lot less hip sway, and Kylie put in an order for food.

"So, what's up with you and Price?" Kylie quickly finished a bird and wrote down its number before setting it aside. She grabbed another paper square, seemingly needing to keep her hands busy.

"He just wanted some help with an English paper." I grabbed one of my now cold fries mulling over the whole thing. Going for sneaky, I casually leaned to the side to check out his table.

All the guys huddled together watching something on a phone, as the girls talked amongst themselves. They munched on carrot sticks someone had smuggled in and looked bored. Emily's eyes cut to me, and with another sneer, she rubbed Garrett's shoulders and whispered something to him.

"Incoming," I whispered and pulled out my phone, trying to act nonchalant. Emily had gotten up and was now coming our way, looking ready to throw down.

The click of heels stopped at our table, and the tension in the air was so thick it was nearly hard to breathe. Kylie and I decided to ignore her in hopes she'd walk away. My reason being she had the power to break someone socially, and Kylie just didn't care what Emily had to say.

"Look, don't get it in your head that just because Garrett talked to you, you're now allowed to be seen with us or anything. He just needed some lackey to help with schoolwork or whatever." Emily waited for her words to sink in, and when it became apparent we weren't going to say anything, she turned to leave with a satisfied smile. I let out a breath and silently thanked whoever was listening that Kylie held her tongue. Unfortunately, I'd spoken too soon.

Emily didn't get two steps away from the table before Kylie started laughing. And not the slow laugh that built into something long and loud. Oh no, this was a loud, can't breathe, hold your gut, wipe tears from your eyes laugh. The kind of laugh that drew all the eyes in a room to land on you.

Backtracking, Emily leaned down and placed both hands on our table, and if I thought the air was thick before, that was nothing compared to the anger floating off Emily now. Flaming crimson spotted her perfectly bronzed cheeks, offsetting the golden goddess tan she must have paid for. "Something funny?" Teeth gritted with a voice full of hard edges and anger-filled, I thought I could see a tick just above her eye starting to jump.

After Kylie wiped her eyes and the chuckling slowed down, she sighed and looked over Emily from head to toe, seemly taking in everything about her. "You're a cliché, a real walking, talking cliché." The ten pounds of makeup didn't hide the confusion on Emily's face.

Taking pity on her, she patted Emily's hand like a child and let out a long sigh. "A cliché is, and I quote," Kylie held up a hand, index finger pointed, and tongue stuck out slightly like she did when trying to recall something difficult. "A phrase and or opinion that is overused and betrays a lack of original thought. You're the cheerleader cliché sweetheart, and to be honest, you should be ashamed." Patting Emily's shoulder with sympathy, Kylie went back to her paper squares like she didn't just drop a truth bomb.

It took a minute for her words to sink in, but I could tell when they did. Emily's face turned so red, no amount of make-up could have hidden it. I honestly thought she'd explode from the pressure in her head. But after taking a calming breath, Emily smiled sweetly, but it was full of loathing. "At least I'm not a pink-haired freak." The words hissed at

Kylie with a sticky sweetness, but they missed their mark judging by Kylie's snort.

"And being a bleach blonde fake would be better?" Kylie stared at Emily's chest when she said the word fake, then dismissed her with a wave of the hand and went back to making paper birds. Staring daggers at the top of Kylie's head, Emily shrieked and stomped back to her table in an infuriated huff.

"Why'd you have to do that?" Resting both arms on the table, I hid my face and groaned. "Why must you antagonize?" I wasn't sure Kylie heard my muffled words till she answered.

"You can't let people talk down to you, buttercup. I mean, really, that was just rude." She numbered another bird then put it away as the waitress dropped our food off. "Here, drink this, you'll feel better."

I peered over my arms and spied a strawberry shake, and nearly all was forgiven. Nearly. The bell over the door rang, and the football team left with bags of take-out and the tribe of girls walking out behind them. Garrett turned and waved back at me with a smile, and Emily sneered. It looked like I made an enemy. Lucky me.

"Ever wonder if her mother told her if she keeps making that face it will get stuck that way." I snorted at Kylie's comment and took a sip of my shake, mood already lighting.

"Are you sure that didn't already happen?" I plucked the cherry from my cup and listened to Kylie laugh like a normal human being as I tried to tie the cherry stem in my mouth. The diner was quiet again, and I was thankful for it.

"So spill. What's really up with you and Garrett?" Kylie grabbed a cold fry, dipped it in the ranch dressing, and munched. I pushed the basket closer to her as I thought back to this morning.

"Like I said, he just wanted help with a paper." Shrugging, I spat out the tied stem and sipped my shake as Kylie switched topics going on about drama class. The same old drama, just new people causing it.

We spent the better part of an hour talking, but I finally had to get home and get some school work done. I waved goodbye to Kylie as we both set off different ways. Before she got too far, I turned and yelled at her. "I think your hair looks amazing pink." She kept on walking but punched a fist in the air and gave me a thumbs up. Whether she wanted to admit it or not, words hurt, and she was not immune to them.

I heard my phone ping and fished it from a back pocket. The screen lit up with a message from The Amazing Garrett. Smiling like an idiot, I read the short text that simply said, *Had fun talking.*

That's it? Well, I guess it was the thought that counted, right? Anyway, he texted me. One of the most popular guys in school texted me, and we had fun together. That same butterfly feeling settled in my stomach, and I couldn't help the smile that stretched farther across my face.

Texting back, I tried to keep it simple with *me too* and a smiley face. I didn't want to seem too eager or try too hard. Floating on cloud nine, I felt like dancing all the way home. I wouldn't, though. That was more of a Kylie thing, but I felt good and was excited for tomorrow and what it could bring.

Chapter 4
Friendship increased by two points.

Walking into the house, I kicked my flip-flops off and put them with the other shoes in the hall box. "I'm home." I didn't hear anyone reply, but that wasn't uncommon. Heading for the kitchen, I heard dad talking in his office, so I made a detour to see what he was up to.

Dad sat in his chair, staring out the window as he talked on the phone. I listened to him for a minute before knocking on the door frame, letting him know I was there. Even though he'd been released for medical reasons, my dad was still a Marine through and through.

He waved at me and kept chatting with mom as I plopped down in one of the soft chairs letting my backpack hit the floor. "Tell her to bring home pizza." He conveyed the message with a smile and talked a minute more before ending the call.

He laid the phone on his lap and rolled to the desk, settling the wheelchair in place before locking it in. After a few clicks on the computer, I had his full attention. "How was school, June Bug?"

"Eh, same thing different day." My cell pinged, so I pulled it from my pocket and checked the notification.

"That's it, no big life revelation or teen drama to talk to your old man about?" Hearing the humor in his voice, I gave him a look and poked at my phone.

"You're not that old." I put the phone away and grabbed my pack from the floor. "So, what did Mom say about pizza?"

"She's working late, so we're on our own." He tossed his phone on the desk, and it slid on some papers.

"So, we're going to starve?" I stood, pulled the backpack higher over my shoulder, and leveled Dad with another look. He knew I couldn't cook, and he wasn't much better.

"I think I still have some MREs if you're brave enough." At my appalled look, he chuckled and rummaged through the desk drawers. "Delivery it is, then." With a smile, he called up a pizza place, and I thanked the heavens I didn't have to choke down a 'meal ready to eat.' Those things were so gross; I didn't know how anyone could eat them. I shook the bag at my father, and he got the message. Waving me off, he ordered a pineapple pizza, and I cringed. Hopefully, he ordered more than just that nasty thing.

After I plopped down on my bed, I unlocked my cell and sent Jeremy an invite to dinner. It didn't take long to get a reply. *If pizza is involved, you can always count me in.* Scoffing at his reply, I switched apps and opened my SocialCircle.

A new friend request tag was blinking, so I poked around and saw that Garrett asked to friend me. With the feeling of butterflies tapdancing, I accepted the friend request and tried not to let this giddy feeling consume me. He just wanted help with English class after all.

But a little part of me wanted it to be more. With a sigh, I tossed the phone aside and started my homework. Time to focus and try not to think about how amazing I would look wearing Garrett's football jersey.

THE DOORBELL RANG SOMETIME later, and when I got to the door, I could hear Jeremy trying to relieve the pizza guy of his burden. I opened the door, and Jeremy breezed in holding the boxes. "Hi, sweetness, pay the man, will ya." He inhaled the smell coming from the boxes and groaned. "Pizza should be its own food group, don't you think?" Without waiting for an answer, Jeremy kicked off his shoes and walked into the dining room.

I paid the man and grabbed some napkins and plates from the kitchen and yelled for Dad to come and get it. "Missed you at school today. How're the allergies?" Settling in a chair, I grabbed a slice and picked a random pepperoni off my cheese pizza, gave it a death glare, then handed it over to Jeremy.

"Well, obviously, I'll live." Taking the disgusting bit of meat from me, Jeremy popped it into his mouth and moaned at how amazing it was. I grabbed a napkin, balled it up, and threw it at his head. Jeremy ducked to the side and avoided getting hit. My aim was off, and I missed by a mile.

"I know my daughter didn't just throw that napkin because I taught her how to throw, and that was just pathetic." Dad rolled into the dining room and leaned down to pick up my napkin. He looked at it then to me with mock disappointment. "How's it going, Jeremy?" Parking at the head of the table, Dad pulled a pizza box toward himself and grabbed a slice.

"It's all good, Mister Jones. Thanks for the dinner invite, by the way. My mother's on this weird, all green food diet. I swear the only thing in the house that's even remotely edible is some out of date crackers in the cabinet." Jeremy shuddered as he grabbed another slice.

"Not a problem," Dad said with a chuckle. "In fact, that reminds me of a time in the corps when my CO found a sock under someone's bunk that was growing this weird green stuff and..."

———————

I PICKED UP THE PIZZA boxes and left the guys in the dining room talking about cars and started packing the leftovers in plastic bags. Folding the cardboard boxes, I put them in the recycling under the cabinet and dusted off both hands.

"Your dad's got some great stories." Jeremy hopped up on the counter and started to nibble on pizza crust and played with his phone. His brown hair fell into his face, most likely blocking his view of the phone. Running a hand through the unruly curly mess did nothing to tame his 'do' into line.

Leaning against the cabinet, I surveyed my friend. "Have you ever thought about getting this thing called a haircut?"

"And let some unknown cut this amazing show of personality?" Running a hand through his hair again, Jeremy leveled me with a look. "I think not." His shirt was a picture of a game I wasn't familiar with and said, *'Speedy thing goes in, speedy thing goes out.'*

"Whatever you say. Here, you need this more than I do." I handed him some of the bagged pizza along with some cookies Mom made earlier that day.

"You're a true friend." He hopped off the counter and hugged the food close. "Food added to inventory, friendship increased by two."

"All that food and our friendship only increased by two points?" Resting both hands on my hips, I tapped a foot and waited for his reply.

But Jeremy just shrugged unfazed at my fake outrage. "Don't hate the player, hate the game."

I grabbed a dishtowel and made like I was going to chuck it at him, but he was already out the door. "Thanks again, Pays. You're the best." Grumbling under my breath, I took some cookies for myself and headed upstairs.

Once again, I sat on the bed with books and papers. I had two essays to write and work for the library to get done. I loved working with the kids on Saturday; it was one of my favorite parts of library work. This week it was my turn for storytime, and I had something special planned for all the kids.

I heard my phone ping and had to move most of the books and papers to find the thing. The Amazing Garrett. *Is Saturday study time good for you?*

I sent a text back explaining I was free any time after noon and set the phone aside. I wasn't going to stare at it until I got a reply, there was homework to do after all.

And it's a good thing I didn't waste my time, because as I got ready for bed, the phone still hadn't buzzed. And as I turned off the bedside light, a little disappointment bloomed in my gut.

Chapter 5
I'd join your revolt.

———

Shutting my locker, I slung my backpack over a shoulder and headed for the lunchroom. I fought the flow of people leaving, weaving in and out of the crowd. Now that we could eat off school grounds, more people left and got food off-campus, and I was perfectly happy with them all leaving.

"Wait up." Nancy fought her way through the crowd heading my way. "Hey." She wheezed as I pulled the lunchroom door open for her. A bit of concern fluttered in my gut, but before I could ask, Nancy spotted Kylie, waved at her, then made a beeline for the food line.

Speed walking ahead of Nancy, I picked up a tray only to hand it to her, but I didn't let go until she looked at me. Clearly, she didn't want to do this here, but I asked anyway. "Anything going on with you?" I threw the question out there lightly, letting her decide if she wanted to lean on me some.

"Nah, but I've heard about fifteen different interesting things about you." Nancy took the tray and grabbed a salad, fries, and a bottle of water before I could put any of that together into a coherent thought.

"What's that supposed to mean?" I picked up an apple, and a pre-made sandwich along with a bottle of water then followed Nancy down the line.

"I just heard from the gossip grapevine someone's making a move on fall queen this year." Nancy paid for her lunch and left me with a grin that seemed a little lighter than before.

"Wait, say what?" I took out my wallet and paid then followed her to our table. At my usual spot, I set the tray down, but I was way more interested in what Nancy had to say than food. "What are you talking about? I never said I was going to the dance."

"Oh, you told her. I wanted to do that." Kylie crossed both arms and glared at Nancy. With a shrug, Nancy stabbed her salad and took a large bite as if a pouting Kylie didn't affect her.

"Will someone please tell me something?" I hissed at them both, but they weren't scared.

Kylie bounced in her seat and pushed some bright pink hair behind an ear. "So everyone knows you and Garrett were talking yesterday. And now people think you're trying to take the crown from miss thing." With a sigh and an eye roll, I could guess she was talking about Emily.

"But that's not the most interesting story floating around." Nancy cut-in pointing her fork in my direction. "Some think you're trying to start a student uprising. Because Garrett is student body whatever and you're you." With another shrug and stab at her salad, Nancy looked like she was having fun with this whole thing.

"Oh, let's do that. I call vice president or beta if we're going to use alphabetic terms. Being that you're an English geek and all that." Kylie clapped her hands and bounced like a child on a sugar high.

"We are not starting an uprising of any kind. Besides, what would we rebel against?" I took a chip from Kylie's tray and watched her think.

"How about the unjust size of school cake?" Nancy poked her fork at the prepackaged cake on Kylie's tray. Okay yeah, I'll give her that. It was small.

"Yes, see. We can totally get other people behind this. Cake for everyone!" Kylie declared a little loud. Some people turned our way, but once they saw it was someone from drama class, they went back to their own thing and ignored us.

Giving them both my best no-nonsense stare, I grabbed my water bottle and twisted the cap off. "One, the cake is a lie. Jeremy told me. Two, an uprising sounds like a lot of work, and I haven't got time for that. Besides, who'd join this party of three anyway?"

"I would; it sounds kind of fun." I sputtered, trying to regain control of my breathing. Garrett patted my back gently; his warm hands didn't help on the normal breathing front. "I wanted to ask if you'd come to lunch with me." Turning, I peered up at him and couldn't tell if he was serious or not.

"Of course, she would." Pulling my tray away, Nancy smiled and bit into my apple. We've been friends for years, so I saw through her scheme. She wanted to get rid of me, so I couldn't ask her any more questions. And like a bad friend, I forgot my concern for her and stood when Garrett pulled me up.

He led me to the doors, and while we weren't holding hands, it seemed like everyone watched us walk out of the lunch hall. Glancing back before the door swung closed, I caught Kylie's eyes, and she silently mouthed the word revolution, then waved her fingers at me, overjoyed at how uncomfortable I clearly was.

Walking down the hallway with Garrett made me feel like I was breaking some kind of unspoken rule. I'd yet to have lunch off school grounds. I could like everyone else, but I'd never seen the reason to. The school lunch wasn't that bad, after all.

Jeremy ambled to the lunchroom wearing the normal gamer shirt and baggy jeans. With his face locked on his phone screen, I didn't have time to warn him before Garrett shoulder-checked him as we hurried by. "Watch where you're going." Garrett dragged me down the hall, and all I could do was give Jeremy a helpless glance before we disappeared down another hallway.

Chapter 6
Lunch with the guys.

———

S itting in Garrett's jacked-up white truck, I rubbed my head and turned down the blaring rap song.

"Not a Fifth Zone fan?" He stopped at a red light and then glanced over at me.

"Nah, more into Hip-Hop Anonymous than anything." I watched the traffic go by as we waited for the light to change. I could feel Garrett's eyes on me, and it left me unnerved, like he was trying to figure me out somehow. "Greenlight." Humming under his breath, he started forward, and soon we were parked at Charlie's.

I slid from the truck and walked around the front. Garrett and I crossed the nearly full parking lot, and anxiety hit hard. He opened the diner door, backed up, and with a sweeping wave, waited for me to head inside.

"Thank you." I muttered the words but didn't think he heard them over all the people rushing around and talking loud. Orders were called out, plates, and cups clanked together. Others I'd seen at school laughed and talked too loud. Unsure where to sit, I felt stuck in place. Feeling a hand on my lower back, I jumped forward and bumped into a diner worker.

Balancing the plates and cups stacked precariously high with practiced care, she recovered and gave me a strained smile. "Sorry." I called after her, but she'd already gone to the back and didn't seem to have heard or cared for my apology.

"Jumpy much? This way." Garrett took my hand and walked down the row of booths filled with people from school. The farther we walked, the quieter the room became. I could still hear some whispered words. But they were just quiet enough I couldn't discern the meaning. The message was clear, though. Shock and surprise that I was with Garret.

"There he is, you're late." Wyatt tossed a fry at Garrett, who ducked the flying potato. It missed him but caught me in the face. "Sorry, Paisley. Didn't see ya there." Pushing his hat up to look at me, Wyatt gave me a welcoming smile and munched on a fry.

Quickly rubbing salt and grease from my face, I shrugged and tried to play the moment off. "It's fine." Shifting weight from foot to foot, I pulled my hand from Garrett's as he sat down. I slid into the booth next to him, and they all started talking about football. Thankful the awkward moment was gone, I watched everyone as they talked and mostly kept to myself.

"What will ya have?" The waitress popped her gum loudly and started taking orders. Most of the guys had glasses of water and chicken salads, except Wyatt, who mixed fries in his salad. Garrett quickly explained it's about eating cleanish for football, Wyatt just harrumphed and asked for more fries to add to his salad.

I waited for Garret to order than placed mine. "I'll have a burger with extra bacon, cheese, and jalapeno. And can you make the bacon extra crispy?" She popped her gum again and gave me a nod before walking off to put our order in. Realizing the table had gone silent, I turned and found everyone staring at me. "What?" Heat started to flood my face at all the attention.

"Love a girl who can eat." Wyatt leaned back in the booth and rubbed a foot against mine. Jerking my feet back, I tucked them safely under my side of the booth and glared at him. But he just grinned like he was having fun messing with me and ate another fry.

"What are you doing here?" Emily's hostile tone cut through the air, and the noise level in the diner dropped as people readied themselves for a showdown of sorts. Standing by our booth in her red pointy heels and plaid short skirt, I glanced up at her and for once didn't feel the need to cower. I had been invited, and she couldn't tell me to leave.

"Paisley's going to help me with some school work, so I thought I'd take her to lunch as a small thank you." Garrett rested an arm behind me on the back of the booth as I fidgeted with the paper napkin.

"But, now, there's not enough room for everyone." Emily crossed both arms and fluttered her eyes lashes at Wyatt. "Be a dear and move."

Popping his hat up, Wyatt gave Emily a once over, stopping at her chest for a long moment. "Nah, pull over a chair, or sit somewhere else."

Emily's face turned red at the dismissal. She stomped a foot and marched away like the child she was acting like. The other girls followed in her wake but snickered behind hands.

"Man." Garrett stretched the word out and rubbed his temple like he could already feel a headache forming. "Why you'd do that?" Thumping his head on the back of the booth, he sighed long and deep.

Ignoring Garrett, Wyatt looked at me, and for the first time, I saw open honesty. "I heard what your friend said the other day. And she's right. Emily acts like a diva and gets prissy when she doesn't get her way." There wasn't any more time for talk as the waitress came around with our food.

I ate and listened to the guys talk football. Garrett tried to get me involved in the conversation, but I knew next to nothing about sports.

Some guy named Liam asked me about a book from the library, and we spent the next twenty minutes talking about poetry. A jock with a brain for poetry, who would have thought. Of course, that was very judgmental of me. Overall, I liked hanging out with the guys, and it ended way too soon.

Back at school, Garrett and the other guys headed for their next class, while I walked with Liam to math. He didn't talk much but was super polite, opening the classroom door for me.

I sat next to Kylie and grabbed some books and a pen from my backpack, which she kept up with because she's an amazing friend like that. A small plane made of origami paper landed lightly on my desk, and I didn't have to wonder who sent it my way. When I unfolded the thing, the word revolution was written in bold pink font. I crumpled it and tossed it back at Kylie, who looked anything but innocent.

The teacher walked into the room and started the lesson, but my thoughts weren't on math. My thoughts were consumed with deep blue eyes and the amazing time I had at lunch.

Chapter 7
Garrett

Watching Paisley chatting with the guys was great. She was so at ease with herself and her love of English words. There was no need to try to impress them or lean over and catch their attention with a low cut shirt. She simply impressed them with her mind. Paisley didn't pretend to be something she wasn't, and in the back of my mind, in a very small part, in the farthest back of my head, I hated her for that.

No, that doesn't sound right. Paisley is great, funny, smart, and well-spoken most of the time. She's definitely not a girl I would have even talked to before. Before what, though. Shaking the thought from my head, I made my way to football practice.

I cracked my knuckles and couldn't help but think back to lunch. Shoving the locker room door open, I waved to a few of the guys who were in various state of dress.

"So you and Paisley, huh?" Wyatt took off his hat and placed it in the locker shelf with the utmost care, then he pulled off his shirt, balled it up, and tossed it inside the locker.

"Yeah, I think so." Pulling my shirt off, I tossed it in the locker then unbuckled my belt. "I'm going to ask her out tomorrow." My insides loosened at that thought, and I felt lighter after saying it, like this odd pressure was now gone from my shoulders.

"Cool. She's nice." I let his comment hang there without replying. I didn't really care what he said or even how he felt about the matter. We finished getting ready in silence and headed out to the field with the others.

Asking her out felt right. Yes... Asking her out was the right thing to do. But for now, I had to get my head in practice mode and clear my mind of her smiling face.

Chapter 8
Friend or foe?

I couldn't breathe. Doubling over, I sucked in some air and continued laughing.

"The true key to any golf game is to sneak up on the ball and hit it as hard as you can." Jeremy crept closer to the light blue ball, gave a loud war cry, and smacked the thing as hard as he could.

The ball hit a tree, bounced off a large decorative rock, then rebounded off a plastic zebra and headed back toward us. Once back on the ugly green felt, the ball rolled to the hole and stopped just an inch from going in. Jeremy turned and gave us both a bow. "And that, ladies, is how it's done."

"No way. You cannot be that good." Kylie stomped over and hip-bumped Jeremy out of the way. "Watch and be amazed." Concentrating on the bright pink ball, Kylie poked her tongue out and tapped the pink orb with the putter sending it down the felt. It bounced off a side bumper and hit Jeremy's ball, knocking it into the hole. Kylie fell to her knees and cursed the golf gods, crying out in the unfairness of it all, while Jeremy did some goofy happy dance.

I placed my neon green ball on the tee and carefully thought through the putt. While Jeremy and Kylie argued about putting technique, I smiled and gave the ball a light tap. It rolled down the felt and into the hole, leaving Kylie's ball alone up-top. "Face it, Kylie, your talent is just not on the green."

"I'll show you talent." Holding her putter like a club, Kylie stomped toward me. I shrieked and took off for the next tee. As Kylie attempted to line up her next shot, I made funny faces doing my darndest to distract her. My phone pinged, so I dug it out of a back pocket and checked the messages.

I muttered a curse and tossed my putter to Jeremy, which he fumbled and nearly dropped his own putter. "I forgot to turn in my timecard. I gotta go."

"Do you want me to drive you over?" Both clubs now rested over his shoulder as he waited for my reply. Kylie screeched as she teed off, giving Jeremy's method a try but ended up sending her ball over the bumpers and into the small creek that ran through the golf range.

"Nah, but thanks, it's not far. Catch ya later." I waved then took off at a jog toward the gate. I blamed the absent-mindedness on Liam. If he hadn't caught me at my locker and asked about ordering books, I totally would have remembered it.

"Hey!" Kylie yelled and waved. "Don't forget about my rehearsal tomorrow. You promised to help with decorations."

I groaned inwardly and waved, letting her know I heard then ran for school. Hopefully, I could make it before they closed for the day.

Running up the school's front steps, I sent a silent prayer of thanks that it was early fall. If it had been summer, I would be dead from heatstroke. Maybe I should have taken Jeremy up on his offer.

Finally, I made it up the steps and grabbed the door handle. Yes! The door opened, and I inwardly danced for joy. My flip-flops slapped the floor and echoed in the deserted hallway. At my locker, I fumbled the lock combo and had to start over. Once I got the locker open, I dug around inside for the timecard and found it folded up in a science book.

Heading for the library, I passed one of the cleaning crew and flashed him my card. Not that he seemed to care. Waving me off, he went back to mopping and listening to music, which was turned up a little too loudly for ear safety.

After knocking on Miss Miller's door, I heard her soft "enter," and after taking a calming breath, I walked in. Miss Miller was everything you'd expect in a school librarian but more. In a bright lime tweed coat and big purple glasses that rested on the end of her nose, she was, without a doubt, the coolest librarian that had ever walked the halls of Willow Creek High.

Even in her seventies with hair long gone grey, she still rocked the vibrant hippie look. I even heard she had some ink, not that she ever admitted it to me, of course.

"So sorry I'm late with this. I got distracted and totally spaced on it." Handing over my card, I took in the mess she called a desk; papers, books, folders, and envelopes covered the surface. She swore she knew where everything was, though.

"Not a problem, dear. I know you teens have a lot going on." She put my card in a stack and started digging in another. "Why back when I was your age, let me tell you I was one busy lady."

"Oh yeah, doing what?" I stretched the last word and rested a hip on her desk as I crossed both arms. Me and Nancy had a bet between the two of us. Try and pin down who Miss Miller really was. She was way too lively and secretive to be just a high school librarian.

"Oh, well." Red stained her cheeks, and I leaned in, not wanting to miss anything. "A story for another time, off with you." She waved a hand

and shooed me away. "I'm sure you have better things to do than be here."

I raised both hands in defeat and started to walk back to the door. "All right, catch ya later, Miss M." Once outside, I picked another daisy and started pulling the petals off absentmindedly.

"He loves me." I flicked the petal aside and picked another. "He loves me not." Continuing the process until once again, I was left with only one petal. "He loves me." I muttered the words like a small prayer and tossed the bald stem aside.

Doing the same with my silly thoughts, I turned my mind to things I had to get done. Lists filled my head, and all thoughts of Garrett and my silly little wish were soon forgotten.

I stopped at the store and picked up a few things for dinner, along with a thing or two not on my mother's list. One does not simply go to the store and not get some Jojo fish.

"You're Paisley, right?" Looking over my shoulder, I saw one of the girls from the cheer squad. Dirty blonde hair in a ponytail, light wash jeans with holes in one knee, and a striped blue shirt. She held bread and dish soap in one hand and balanced some kind of fashion magazine in the other.

"Uh, yeah, and you are?" I adjusted my stuff and turned to face her better. Come to think of it; I saw her yesterday at the diner. Oh joy, this may not be good.

"Mandy, I'm the second on the cheer squad. And I got to say; it's nice to meet someone who can take Emily down a peg or two."

Taken back by her statement, I stared at her in bewilderment. Mandy laughed at my expression, and the sound of it was just like a Disney princes come to life. I half expected woodland animals to walk in the store and do her bidding at any moment.

"Oh my gosh, calm down, you look horrified. Relax, I just wanted to chat. That's all, I swear." Mandy flipped some hair back and smiled, but her words didn't comfort me much.

"About what?" I narrowed my eyes at her and tried to get a better read on what kind of a person she was. I mean, in all actuality, she could be Emily's spy searching for some kind weakness. But then again, I could just be a little overly dramatic.

Mandy shrugged in dismissal and shifted her groceries. "Oh nothing much, give me your number, we can do a girl coffee date of sorts." She pulled a cell from her purse and waited for my number.

I just didn't have the heart to tell her no. So I gave it to her and promised we'd do coffee or something this week. Huh, looked like I might have made a new friend. As she left for the checkout, the thought made me laugh out loud. I got a few weird looks for it, but I mean, really, who just randomly starts talking to someone in the store and becomes friends? Sounded like something from a book or movie.

While I waited in the checkout line, my phone pinged. Mandy had sent me a friend request on my SocialCircle. I accepted, and because there was the time, I creeped on her page a few minutes while waiting for the line to move. She had posted a lot of pictures of her and Emily. If I had to guess just by pics alone, they must have been good friends. I'd have to be on guard just in case she really was a spy. Mentally I rolled my eyes; I had started to sound overly dramatic like Kylie.

I scrolled again as the line moved and found other pictures from cheer camp. Random coffee selfies took up most of her page, along with some generic inspirational quotes. I texted Kylie and asked what she thought about the whole thing but knew I might not get a reply until tomorrow.

On the way home, I found another daisy and started picking the petals. I went through all the little white petals until I was left with one. "He loves me." Scoffing, I tossed the stem away as I climbed the front steps to the house. And again, I was struck with how much I wished it could be as easy as that.

Chapter 9
It was just a little paint.

———

I grabbed another brush, popped off the lid from the black paint, and added some detail lines to the tree I'd been working on for the last hour. Exciting stuff. I half-listened to Kylie as she rehearsed lines and watched the others around me do the same. From my place on stage, I could see that the school's theater was full of people auditioning for this year's big play. I didn't care for this kind of thing, but my best friend did, so I was there to support her.

"Nice tree, creative skills increased by three." Jeremy plopped down beside me and pulled out his phone.

"Just three, that's a solid five-point tree." I faked outrage at the low point score Jeremy gave my tree. I'd been working on it for so long, and it was worth more than a measly three points.

"Nope, if it were a happy little tree, it'd be would totally be worth five points. But that just one sad-looking thing." No longer playing outraged, I assessed my painting skills, and okay yeah, maybe he had a point. It was a poor excuse for a tree. I hadn't waited long enough for it to dry, and now my black lines smeared with the green paint. But hey, I'm an English major, not an artist.

"Everyone's a critic." Muttering under my breath, I crossed my legs and leaned back and watched everyone go about working. Plenty of people sat in the theater seats and ran through lines. Some overacted, while others sat quietly and read to themselves. Apparently, a big shot Broadway guy was coming down to see people perform, and it was a very big deal. "How;s your game going?" Jeremy's shoulders slumped, and I felt bad for asking.

"Granny B just leveled up and got the quest sword we've been after for two weeks. For someone in her eighties, she's ruthless when it comes to gameplay." Jeremy's grandmother was crazy but in a good way. She was the one who taught him D&D in the first place. When I'm her age, I only hope I'm half as amazing as her.

Kylie sat with a huff and started bouncing like a kid on a sugar high. "I'm so nervous I could puke." She wrapped both arms around herself and started humming like she was meditating.

"Have you tried, not being nervous?" Jeremy looked over the top of his phone at Kylie with an uplifted brow.

"Oh, wow, I'm cured. Why didn't I think of that before?" She fell back onto the floor, spread out like a starfish, and bellowed, "Come one, come all and see Jeremey for all that ails you." She received a few weird looks, but overall, not many people seemed to care that Kylie had just yelled something random.

"Speech points increase to seventy-two." Jeremy went for a high five, but Kylie kicked his hand away with a disgusted scoff.

"I was being facetious, you nitwit."

My phone pinged, and I left them to argue, checking the notification. The Amazing Garrett. *Where you at?* Not able to stop a smile, I stared at the screen like a nut.

"Who texted you?" Kylie leaned in and tried to catch a glimpse of the screen, but I hugged it close, hiding it from her snooping.

"No one." Even I heard the high false note in my voice.

"Liar liar, face on fire." Moving faster than ever, Kylie grabbed my phone and took off across the stage before I could stop her.

"Hey, give that back!" We zig-zagged around the props, people, and paint. I nearly got taken out by the lighting guy and had to do a quick limbo matrix style to keep my head in place.

Finding Kylie halfway across the stage with a cat-that-ate-the-canary-grin, I took the phone back, but before I could lay into her about being a phone thief, Miss Armod caught up with us.

"Girls, how many times must I tell you, the theater is a serious place and demands respect as such." Tall and thin, Miss Armod had a head full of grey hair, which she was very proud of. Today it was styled in a bun with a pair of large orange glasses resting on the crown of her head. In the same way, her clothes were always busier than a bar on Friday night. She commanded your attention because she expected nothing less. I sometimes jokingly told Kylie if she didn't make it big, she'd turn into someone just like Miss Armod.

Muttering an apology didn't seem to appease the drama teacher, so we had to stand there and listen to her go on about the proper respect the theater is due. My phone pinged, but I didn't dare look at it. Finally, after what seemed like hours, she got called away to deal with a prop issue, and both of us let out a deep sigh relief.

"She's a bit much, huh." Garrett stood not far from us with Wyatt, who was on his phone, not paying attention to anything around him.

"Miss Armod is a being unto herself." I fiddled with the end of my shirt looking anywhere but at him.

"Well, I have to practice my lines. Bye." Skipping off in pure Kylie fashion, she left me awkward silence.

"You know what, as much fun as this whole thing looks to be, I'm out." With a tip of his hat, Wyatt strolled away but didn't get far. Stopping to chat with some drama girls in short shorts, I could see his charming grin from here. I finally glanced over at Garrett, trying with all my might to come up with something clever to say.

Garrett shook his head and smirked at me. "I didn't have practice today, so figured I'd hang out here with you. If that's cool." He stepped a bit closer, and we were just a foot apart.

"Yeah sure, I mean, we're just painting and getting things ready for the fall play. More work than fun." I said with an apologetic smile. Running both hands down my pants, I racked my brain for something funny to say, but nope, my brain failed me again.

"Hanging with you is always fun." Garrett pulled me to his side and rested an arm over my shoulders. "So, what do we do first?"

"Uh, I guess we can finish painting some trees." I noted people watching us so slid out from under his arm and put a little space in between us.

Getting back to Jeremy, I found him off his phone and painting a trunk of a tree. "Since you're tall, you can paint the top." Pointing to the tree, I handed Garrett a brush and checked on my sad tree. It needed to dry more, so I went to find another tree or bush cutout.

Lifting the wooden cutout was a bit hard, not that it was heavy or anything, more like blocky and hard to handle. "Let me get that." Jeremy gently pushed me aside, then grabbed the cutout, and took it back to where I'd been painting.

"Thanks." Grabbing my paintbrush, I noticed the lack of paint. Huh, I knew there was a whole can of green over here somewhere.

The crashing sound of a metal can and cursing filled the overly loud room, and everyone stopped to see what happened. People pointed and laughed as Jeremy flipped his now green hair back and shoved Garrett in the chest. Garrett pushed back, and Jeremy fell in the paint with a splat, spreading green paint over Miss Armod's beloved theater floor.

"What in heaven's name happened here?" Hands on her large hips, Miss Armod appeared and ranted for a moment over the disrespect everyone was showing.

Garrett tossed both hands up and took a step back like he had nothing to do with whatever was going on. "I was just painting, minding my own business, honestly don't know what happened, Miss Armod."

Jeremy tried to stand but slipped and fell to his knees. I hurried over and gave him a hand up. Paint smeared my forearm and hands, but I didn't pay it any mind. Kicking off my flip-flops, I picked them up and kept them turned away from my shirt to lessen the paint transfer.

"Mister Price, please go find a janitor to clean this up immediately. And you, kindly leave this stage. Do not return until you are paint-free." Clapping her hands, Miss Armod tried to restore order to the stage, but teens it seemed will always be jerks. Some took pictures and snickered behind their hands.

"Sorry man, should have watched where you were going." Garrett started to crossed his arms but stopped when he saw the paint there and smirked at Jeremy. Kicking off his shoes, Jeremy didn't say a thing, but he didn't have to for me to know he was angry. "Come on, man, no hard feelings." Garrett held out a hand and tried to make nice, but Jeremy slapped it away without a word and walked off in socked feet.

"Dude, he has some anger issues." Garrett shrugged at the paint spill like it wasn't his problem and then held a hand out for me. "Better go do what she says, come help me find a janitor?" Garrett did a flirty eyebrow lift and graced me with a megawatt smile.

Ignoring him, I picked up Jeremy's shoes then grabbed a brush to try and get as much paint off of them as I could. "Actually, I should bring Jeremy his shoes; he'll need them and all." It was a lame excuse I knew, but I'd never seen him this mad before.

Garrett rocked back on his heels, seemingly a little put out by my refusal. "That's cool. See ya later then." I muttered something noncommittal and walked off with a wave over my shoulder.

It took me a good ten minutes to find Jeremy, which was surprising given the fact he was covered in green paint. He sat on the bed of his truck in the last spot on the lot, rubbing a towel over his head, but it didn't seem to be doing any good.

"Here, I tried to save your shoes." I placed them in the back of the truck and winced at the amount of paint still on them. He had changed into a pair of gym clothes, but green paint still stained ends of his hair. "Well, looks like you need that haircut after all, huh." Flinching at his glare, I felt like a bad friend for making light of the whole thing.

Deploying a tactic my father told me about, I waited and let the warmth of the sun seep through my shoulders and let the quiet linger. Most people can't handle the quiet and felt the need to fill it with noise. Sometimes that noise was just that, noise. Other times it was stuff that's been weighing on them, and they just need someone to be quiet long enough to listen.

"You know he did that on purpose." He gave one last rough scrub through his hair, then gave up on the towel and tossed it behind him where it hit the back window leaving a small smear of paint.

"Accidents happen, and he said he was sorry." With both arms crossed, I shifted my feet and gave it some thought. I hated to think Garrett would do something like that. Why would he? I'd never thought of him as a mean spirited person, but then again, did I really didn't know anything about him.

"Oh, come on, Pays, in case you hadn't noticed, he's a guy, and most guys are jerks. Especially guys like him." Jeremy pointed to the school and glared at me with disdain. I could understand him being upset, but accusing someone of pouring paint on him was a lot to take in.

Wounded at his tone, I backed up and kicked a small rock only to watch as it bounced off the curb and come back at me. I didn't want to meet Jeremy's eyes. I had this sinking feeling he was right. The whole thing made my head ache, so I plucked a flower from nearby and started to pull the petals off.

He loves me. I said it mentally, then flicked the petal aside and went after another petal. *He loves me not.* I continued the process until, once again, I was left with only one petal. *He loves me.*

"First," I said with a newfound conviction. "That's stereotyping and two, why would he want to dump paint on you?" I tossed the stem aside, then planted both hands on my hips and tried to give Garrett the benefit of the doubt.

"Uh, maybe because he likes you, and we're friends, and he doesn't like that." Throwing both hands in the air in a helpless gesture, Jeremy and I seemed locked in a silent battle of wills. A car horn blared, and we both turned to see what was going on.

"Hey, Paisley, need a ride?" Garrett hollered from his jacked-up truck. He leaned out the window and smiled at me.

"I'm telling you, Paisley; he did it on purpose." Jeremy crossed his arms, frowned, and waited for me to believe him. Because that's what a true friend would do.

"It was an accident, Jer. You're just reading too much into it." I took a step back and could read the disappointment on his face. It really was an accident. I was sure of it. "I'll text you later, okay?" Not waiting for an answer, because I honestly didn't want to hear what he had to say, I turned and ran over to where Garrett waited.

Leaning over to the passenger side, Garrett pushed the door open and gave me a smile that melted my brain and made it hard to think. "Get in." I caved like a stack of playing cards and jumped inside without thought.

"Where are we going?" I hung on for dear life as he left the parking lot a little too quick and weaved through traffic at an alarming speed.

"Relax, I'm a great driver." He stopped at a red light and flashed me a smile before turning on the radio.

The rap music was a bit too loud, so I turned it down to a more ear-friendly level as the light changed. "It's not your driving I'm worried about." I tightened the seatbelt and gave him a look, but he didn't catch it.

"Whatever. I wanted to show you something." Pulling onto an old red dirt road we rocked with every pothole, I took in the trees and wooded area so different than the city I was used too. Soon we were really in the forest, and I started to get a bit nervous. All the horror movies I'd watched and warnings from my parents began to fill my head, but I tried to push them aside and think like a rational person.

"My dad used to take me out here to fish when I was younger. But that was a long time ago. Before football and junk." The trees started to thin out as he turned off the road and into the tall grass. The cab rocked for a moment on the uneven ground before he turned the truck around and parked. Without saying anything, he got out and made his way to the tailgate, then started pulling things out.

The long grass tickled my legs as I walked around to join him. "Oh, wow." I gazed over the unruly field; it seemed like you could see forever. The sky was in full bloom with deep reds and golden oranges. I'd never seen color so bright or magnificent. This was something you'd never see in town with all the buildings.

"Up you go." Garrett pulled me over and lifted me onto the tailgate. Jumping up beside me, the truck dipped as his weight settled, then he leaned closer and pointed to a mountain you could just barely see. "That's Seekers Point. You can climb it in the summer. Me and the guys have a time or two." I could barely make out the mountain line in the fading sunlight.

"I didn't know we lived so close to a mountain." Swinging both feet, I took in all the quiet around me and smiled as the lighting bugs started to flutter about in the breeze.

"I'll take ya there sometime, it'll be fun." Garrett leaned back and stretched out on the truck bed with both arms behind his head. His shirt stretched tight over his stomach showing just a hint of skin, not that I was looking or anything.

Sitting there in the peaceful quiet, I felt myself relax. "Can I ask you something?" The thought had been running through my mind for the last half hour, and I needed to know.

"You can ask me anything." Hands still behind his head, Garrett seemed relaxed and more open than I had ever seen him at school.

"Did you dump the paint on Jeremy, like on purpose?" I bit my lip and waited for him to respond. But in the back of my mind, I almost didn't want to hear the answer.

"Is that what you two were talking about?" I nodded and watched his reaction. "I'll apologize again, but I didn't mean too." Accepting his answer, I kicked the tall grass and watched the fireflies flicker around the clearing. I didn't want to argue with him. Not here and now. It was like we were really starting to get to know each other without school or friends in the way.

"Here, lean back, or you'll miss the show." Garrett took my hand, and I let him pull me down beside him. He wrapped an arm around me, and his warmth seeped into my chilled shoulders. "Look." He said and pointed skyward.

The sun was almost down, and you could just start to make out the stars. Thousands of them winked on as it got darker, and soon, the sky filled with little silver lights. "Go out with me tomorrow night?" He said it so quietly I wasn't sure I heard him right. "I mean, if you're free, that is." He tried to sound flippant and make light of the request like he was nervous I'd say no or something.

You got to play it cool here, Pays. Taking an extra second to pretend like I was thinking about it, I simply said sure and felt him relax beside me. Neither of us spoke again after that. We just laid there together and watched the stars shine in the quiet of the woods.

Chapter 10
Coffee with a spy.

———

Mandy had taken at least half a dozen selfies before I got my tea, then a dozen more when the barista handed her a pink drink. And then we had to move to the back of the shop because the lighting was more natural where she took two dozen more before she had a picture worthy of posting. "So, I want all the deets on you and Garrett. And don't even think of leaving out a thing." She sucked down some of her drink and tapped a pastel-colored nail on the table.

I took a sip and stalled for time to mull over how much to tell her. I'd only just got home when she'd texted and wanted to meet up for an evening coffee run. Which gave me an escape from all my mother's probing questions.

"Well, I'm helping him with some school work." Shrugging like it wasn't a big deal, I decided to leave it at that. I wasn't going to give anything away that she could take back to Emily and possibly use it against me.

Leaning in a little closer, Mandy dropped her voice to a whisper, but I could still detect a good bit of glee hiding underneath. "But I saw you eating with him and the guys at the diner, which means he had to have asked you out for lunch, am I right? He hasn't even done that for Emily, and trust me; she's dropped a lot of hints. Gosh, she's still fuming about it." Her eyes sparkled like this was a juicy secret she couldn't keep to herself. "And, you both were seen leaving the parking lot together earlier today. So the question is, where did you two go?" She sipped her drink and looked quite happy with herself. Like she caught me in a lie, and I'd have to answer her questions now.

But I just shrugged and tried to play it off. "We just drove around and talked about nothing." Shifting in my chair, I watched the other people in the small coffee shop, hoping Mandy would drop this line of questioning. I knew some people from the drama club by sight, but they didn't pay us any mind.

"Oh no, you can't pull that with me. I want details." Biting a thumbnail, Mandy looked eager for any dirty laundry. And I wondered briefly why I was even here talking with her.

I drank the last of my tea and once again shrugged. "I can't tell you anything more than what happened. We drove around and then chatted for a little while." Of course, I left out where we went and the fact he'd asked me out. I was keeping the magic of the night to myself thank you very much.

She pouted for a bit, then pulled out a cell and checked her SocialCircle page. "Everyone says Garrett is falling for you, but that's just hearsay. You can never really know what's the truth nowadays, especially with guys. Know what I mean?" She flipped some hair back and kept poking at her phone.

"What do you think the truth is, then?" I posed the question even though I didn't care to know her opinion. I had noticed since Garrett started talking to me, other people I've never spoken to in my whole school life suddenly felt the need to speak with me. People who've completely ignored me now knew my name and the fact I wanted to be a librarian. I'd accepted so many friend requests, it was just getting ridiculous.

Mandy crossed her legs and hummed to herself for a second. Her unseasonably short skirt rode up, showing a lot of skin, not that I think she cared about how much skin was showing. "I think," she said, tapping a finger on her chin. "You're making a move on fall queen and trying to knock Emily down a peg or two for all the times she's been nasty or uppity."

That was so far from the truth; it was hilarious. Come to think of it, Emily had never been mean or nasty to me or anyone that I could think of. Sure she could be unpleasant and uppity, but most people were at some point or another. I fiddled with my cup but didn't answer any more questions, which didn't encourage her to drop the subject.

"I will say this though, if you want to make fall queen, you need to detach yourself from some people. Mainly the nerdy one and the drama club, pink-haired girl. They're both bad for your image." Mandy dropped her wisdom like it was nothing to stop speaking to people you had practically known your whole life.

I must have made a face because Mandy patted my hand and leaned in again. "I know you think they're great people, and they probably are. I'm not arguing that. It's just they're not good to be seen with right now. If they're your true friends, they'll get it and be there when you can hang out again. It's not that big of a deal." With a fake smile, Mandy got up and grabbed her cup. "I'll be right back." Without waiting for a reply, she walked off to the restroom to probably take more selfies.

So, is that was being popular was? Hanging out with people I didn't like and pretending to like people who are jerks? I took my cup to the bar and left it for the barista, all the while letting what Mandy said sink in. Dropping Jeremey and Kylie was just stupid, and I wouldn't do it.

Mandy walked out of the restroom and slung an arm around my shoulder then took a selfie before I could do anything. "You'd make a great fall queen. You just need to lose some baggage for a hot minute. But I can help you with everything else you could ever need. Don't answer now, just think on it."

Making a kissy sound at me, Mandy turned and glided out of the shop with a walk a beauty pageant contestant would be jealous of.

I didn't want to give up my friends for any of this. It wasn't worth it to me. My phone pinged, and I found a text from Garrett. *I've never taken anyone to my spot before. I enjoyed it a lot. We need to do it again. Soon.*

I wrote a simple text back and slipped the phone in my back pocket. Everything Mandy said pulled at my soul at that moment. I didn't want to lose my friends, but the more I heard it and talked about it, the more I liked the idea of Garrett and me.

Mentally tired from Mandy's interrogation, I went through a list of things that had to be done and groaned when I realized school work was at home and waiting. I pulled up Kylie's number, wanting to tell her about today, but I knew she wouldn't be terribly happy for me. Heck, she'd made it no secret she didn't think highly of Garrett. I put the phone away without texting and headed home. I'd tell her later.

Chapter 11
Beer pong anyone?

———

I waved goodbye to both parents and waited until they were halfway down the street before I shut the door and bolted to my room. With ten minutes to spare, I threw clothes out of the closet, looking for just the right thing. Something that said cool without showing too much skin, but something totally different than what I'd normally wear.

In the back of the closet, I found a short denim skirt I'd only worn once and paired it with a low cut purple top. Staring at the person in the mirror, I turned one way, then the other, but something just didn't look right. I pulled my hair up in a topknot and checked my reflection again, but still felt something was off. Garrett hadn't told me where we're going, so I wasn't sure how fancy to dress.

Biting my lip, I took off the skirt and tossed it aside. If we were going on a date, he was going to get the real me, not some fake version. I hurried back to the closet and grabbed some old paint-splattered jeans. Looking more myself, I tossed the shirt and found a band camp tee from years ago that had just the right amount of holes in it.

Happy with how I looked, I put a little bit of makeup, nothing too loud, just some mascara and lip color Kylie insisted I needed in my life. Pulling my hair into its normal ponytail, I called the look done and resisted glancing at the clock on the phone for the nine hundredth time. Scowling at the mess I'd made, I took a few minutes to put everything away to keep my mind busy.

My phone pinged, and I snatched it up, but it wasn't Garrett. I fell on the bed with a sigh and replied to Nancy. We chatted about work schedules and homework, all the while I kept an eye on the clock. He was late.

Feeling like a balloon that had lost all its air, I tossed my phone on the bed and went downstairs to get some munchies. Grabbing some chips and a soda, I seriously thought about calling for a pizza. I mean, pizza had a pretty good track record of never letting me down. Unlike some people who would remain nameless.

Grumbling under my breath, I piled my horde of junk food on the desk, then noticed a little blue notification light blinking on my phone. Dang it, I forgot to reply to Nancy.

A simple *waiting outside* text from Garrett made me squeal like a fangirl who was going to meet her crush in real life. I felt ten feet off the ground as I ran down the stairs and skidded to a stop at the front door.

I did a quick pocket check, phone and house keys, lip balm, and at my dad's insistence, a small can of pepper spray. After slipping my flip flops on, I took a deep breath and calmly opened the front door like a normal human being.

Garrett sat in the large truck playing with his phone, head bobbing to the loud music belting from the speakers. I felt a nervous flutter in my gut but walked down the front walk calmly all the while telling myself over and over to play it cool.

"Hey, I was beginning to wonder." I buckled the safety belt and glanced over at him. He was still on the phone and hadn't said anything yet. Something's was up tonight, but I couldn't put a finger on what. "You okay?" Both of our phones pinged, and I checked mine as he typed a reply on his.

Reading Nancy's text, I cut off our chat by saying homework had to get done and pressed send as Garret chucked his cell in the cup holder where it rattled around. He didn't seem too concerned with breaking the screen.

"Yeah, everything's great." By his harsh tone, it was clear everything wasn't fine. But not knowing him well enough, I wasn't going to call him on the obvious lie. He wore some old faded jeans and a skin-tight black shirt with his hair in a disheveled mess.

A bit uncomfortable with his weird mood, I wasn't sure what to do. Clearly, he didn't want to talk about whatever was bothering him, so we spent the whole drive in silence. Thankfully it didn't take long to get there, wherever there was.

Garrett parked in front of a house that looked like it should have been on a magazine cover. Or it could have been if it wasn't for all the teens hanging off the porch rails with red cups, laughing, and acting a fool.

Awful rap music blared from inside, spilling out the door to a barely tolerable level outside. People were everywhere, in crowds of four or five standing around talking or running around in various states of undress. Either this was a low key pool party, or some people didn't know how to dress appropriately.

Garrett snatched up his abused phone, jumped out of the truck, then walked around and opened my door. I slid out, and as soon as my feet hit the street, I instantly felt the eyes of everyone outside on us. I silently told myself not to fidget or hide behind Garrett in an effort to keep the judgy stares of people off me. Garrett grabbed my hand and pulled me up the walkway.

People stared like the whole outside of the house was playing freeze tag, and we were it. Some even glared before walking off, which was fine by me. They could take their rude selves somewhere else for all I cared.

Whatever spell had been in effect seemed to have broken once Garrett walked into the house. All his problems appeared to melt from his face. He smiled and greeted friends warmly. Fist-bumps and back-slapping bro hugs were exchanged as we made our way deeper into the house that seemed to be filled to the rafters with people.

Somehow, I ended up with a cup of what I'd guessed was some type of alcohol and grimaced at the overly sweet smell. I passed by a table and left the drink there as I tried to follow Garrett. This wasn't my crowd, some I knew from passing in the halls at school, but others I had no idea.

Out on the back deck, there were still too many people, but the music was at a more tolerable level of ear bleedingly loud. Overwhelmed with the number of people, I backed up and leaned against the wall just to get out of the way and have my own space for a bit.

Garrett left me and strolled over to the beer pong table with cup in hand and laughed with friends. If I'd known we were going to a place like this, I would have stayed home with a book and pizza. Heck, I would have rather have done the last of my homework than be here.

Someone shrieked, and the sound of loud splashing accompanied by chanting caught my attention. The pool was filled with people horsing around and somehow, pool noodles seemed to be involved, I definitely wanted nothing to do with any of that.

Some girls waltzed around with little clothing flaunting their flat stomachs and deep tans. How they could wear anything like that this late in the year was beyond me.

Someone bumped into me in their haste to get inside, sending me sideways. Unfortunately, no one can fight gravity and win, including me. I was going down, and it was going to hurt. Or it would have if Wyatt hadn't caught me.

"Hey, watch what you're doing." Wyatt's anger-filled shout followed the guy, but either the dude didn't hear with all the noise, or more likely, didn't care. Leading me away from the door, Wyatt leaned on the porch railing and drank deep from his cup. "I didn't think this was your kind of thing." He tipped his hat to some girls as they walked by without missing a beat. They skipped down the deck giggling only to scream when some guys picked them up and jumped in the pool. At least some people appeared to be enjoying themselves.

"Yeah, you're right, not my thing. Garrett said he was going to take me out. If I had known he meant here..." I let the words hang there as I watched what was going on with a mix of interest and annoyance.

"Garrett can be pretty stupid sometimes." He drank the last of whatever was in the cup, then crushed it and chucked it in the yard. "I'm going after another; you want one?" Wyatt pointed over a shoulder to a table I could just barely see inside. It was full of different colored drinks from bottles of varies sizes.

I declined the offer and crossed my arms. Leaning on the rails, I spotted Emily and her bunch hanging out with Garrett now. Wearing a pink barely-there bikini, Emily leaned on Garrett and whispered something causing him to laugh loudly. Needless to say, I was feeling just a little of that green-eyed monster coming over me.

"Don't let her get to you; try to enjoy yourself. Liam's around here somewhere; you two can talk books or whatever." Wyatt rubbed my shoulder before going in search of something more to drink. He didn't get far before he turned and came back then stared at me for a moment. "If anyone starts bothering you, find me or Liam, okay?" I noticed his concern and appreciated the fact he cared. After a nod of agreement, he turned and left again. I was beginning to think he was a whole lot nicer than he liked to let on.

Surveying the back yard again, I spotted Garrett staring at me frowning, but as soon as we locked eyes, he smiled and waved me over. I forced a smile and set my mind on having a good time. Just because this wasn't my thing, didn't mean I couldn't enjoy time with Garrett.

People had started to crowd around the beer pong table excited about something. Money changed hands, and bets were made. Emily still stood at Garrett's side and gave me the stink-eye when I walked up. I tried not to let her bother me too much. I had just as much right to be here as she did.

"Hey." Garrett pulled me over, and the smell of booze that came off him made my eyes water. I pushed him back and tried to get some space between us, but he leaned in, and I felt a hand resting just above my butt. "I need a second for beer pong, what do you say?" Removing his hand, I stepped back and took in the scene around me. People swayed on unsteady legs and laughed at friends who were just a little too far gone. Would they even remember tonight? Or would it be a large blank spot in their memory?

"Thanks, but I don't drink." More people heard me than I would have liked. Not that I'm ashamed of my choices, but people often made a big deal out of it. And of course, Emily was the kind of person who'd make a big deal out of it.

"What do you mean you don't drink?" Scoffing, she looked around, checking to see how many people could hear her cut me down. "Afraid mommy and daddy will find out." That got people laughing, of course. I crossed my arms and felt a little stupid, more from the fact people were laughing at me than the decision not to drink. It was my choice, and I wouldn't let anyone make me feel bad over it.

"Come on, Paisley. Don't be weird. Have a drink and play with us." Garrett held a ping pong ball out to me, his smile still goofy and relaxed.

And sure, at that moment, I wanted so badly to say yes and play their game. But this was important to me, and I wasn't going to bend on it, no matter how much they picked on me.

"Yeah, Paisley, have a drink." Emily threw a cup at me, which I missed causing the contents to soak my shirt. Now a very see-through shirt. People laughed and pointed. Even Garrett had a chuckle at my expense.

My eyes burned as I turned and pushed people aside, headed for the house. Garrett yelled something, but I didn't stop. I didn't care what he had to say at this point. Kylie was right. Garrett was as shallow as a puddle, and I hated the fact I ever had a crush on him.

Chapter 12
Now that's what I call friendship.

―――

I hid in the bathroom. Lame, I know, but my shirt was soaked and clung to my chest, leaving nothing to the imagination. I put it in the sink and ran water over it trying to get as much of the beer stain off as I could. I grabbed an ornate monogrammed towel from a fancy wicker basket and tried to dry my shirt, but it didn't work well.

Fighting tears, I slid down the wall and called myself ten kinds of stupid. I should have told Garrett to leave when we got here, that parties like this weren't something I wanted to be a part of.

Wiping my eyes, the Imperial March started playing and filled the room with its dark and imposing tune. I pulled the cell from a back pocket and wiped my eyes again. "Hey, Jeremy, what's up?" Someone banged on the door and yelled for me to hurry up, but I ignored them.

"That was my question. You called and never said anything, then hung up." Someone yelled in the background from wherever Jeremy was, and I wondered if I was bothering him.

"Sorry, I think I might have butt-dialed you." Again someone banged on the door, and I yelled for them to chill out. If I wanted to camp out in here the rest of the night, tough luck for them. Wiping my nose on the back of a hand, I rested my head on the wall. "Sorry again, I'll let you get back to whatever you were doing."

"Hey, Pays, are you okay?" Jeremy's words filled with concern made it hard to keep my voice from trembling as my eyes welled again.

"Garrett took me to some party, I have a beer-stained shirt, and everyone laughed at me. Now I'm hiding in the bathroom like a lame-o smelling like beer." With a shuttering breath, I tried to collect myself before I had a total meltdown.

"Stay right there. And keep the door locked." Not waiting for a reply, Jeremy hung up, and I was left there waiting, listening to the awful music that filtered through the door.

After about ten minutes of people banged on the door and ear bleeding music, Jeremy texted.

I'm outside, you want me to come get you, or do you feel comfortable heading out by yourself?

Relief and gratitude washed over me over his unexpected rescue. *I'll be right down, keep the truck running.*

Ringing out my shirt one more time, I slipped it on and shuttered as the wet material stuck to skin. I checked myself out in the mirror and wiped my face for any last streaks of mascara. There was nothing I could do for red eyes.

I flipped the little lock and walked out of the bathroom like I owned the place. When in doubt, pretend you know where you're going.

The hallway was half full of people now, unlike the wall to wall bodies an hour ago. They moved from room to room, laughing and having a good time. Most everyone was wasted and had to use the walls to keep upright.

Walking past a door, I glanced in. The room was heavy with smoke, and several people sat on the floor or laid on the bed, laughing and drinking. I walked past before someone asked me to join them.

I nearly collided into a couple stumbling out of a bedroom and had to back up. Glassy eyes and a goofy grin, the guy had to prop himself on the door frame to keep upright. The girl apologized in a gritty voice and leaned on the guy running both hands up his shirt, which was clearly inside out. I moved past them without saying a thing and hurried down the stairs.

In the living room, someone had turned down the music, and most everyone stood around talking. Some danced if you called what they were doing dancing, more than one couple sat on the couches making out. I'd had more than enough of this place and made a beeline for the door.

I breathed fresh air for the first time in what seemed like hours and pushed my way through the people standing on the front deck. Jeremy was waiting at the curb in his old truck, watching the house. I waved at him and rushed for freedom.

A hand came out of nowhere and grabbed my upper arm, pulling me into a crowd of drunk guys. "Where you off to pretty thing, the party's just getting started." The smell of sweat and alcohol made me want to gag. The clawing feeling of panic started to set in just as I heard Jeremy's voice call my name.

"Oh look, it's the knight in shining armor come to rescue the girl." The guys surrounding me laughed loudly and crowded closer like they were playing some kind of a game with us.

Jeremy didn't seem put off by their comments. Instead, he stood about a foot from the bottom step of the deck, looking not to have a care in the world. I could see the wheels turning as he tried to figure a way out of this without making it a bigger deal or starting a fight over it.

"I'll tell you what," The ring leader pulled me a little closer as he laid down a challenge. "We'll let her go if you can answer our question."

The other seemed to think that was funny and laughed. The guy who had my arm chugged a beer then tossed the can over the rails. Ugh, I hated the smell of that stuff. With an arm around my shoulders now, I couldn't move, and that feeling of panic came over me again with a vengeance.

With a simple shrug, Jeremy shoved both hands deep in his pockets. "Just one question?"

"Yeah, smart guy. Just one." The ring leader leaned down and rested his forearm on the handrail pulling me with him in an uncomfortable manner. "What is the number of Pi?" Unable to keep a straight face, the guy burst into laughter. The others standing around joined the laughter. Jeremy seemed unfazed and started up the deck.

"Actually, that can be explained very easily. May I see your phone?" Without waiting for a reply, Jeremy grabbed one of their cells and tapped on the surface. Soon a lady started singing, and the phone was handed back to the guy.

I leaned in and saw a scantily clad woman singing about the numbers in Pi. All the guys crowded around to get a better look at the phone, forgetting all about me. Jeremy grabbed my hand, and we eased away from them slowly.

Once off the deck, we broke into a run for the waiting truck. Slamming the doors, Jeremy peeled out of there before they even knew what happened. I couldn't help the laugh that bubbled out of me. Once I could breathe again, I gave Jeremy a long look.

Sensing my gaze, he turned to face me but not for long. Jeremy was always a cautious driver and kept his eyes on the road and hands at ten and two. "What?"

"Do I even want to know where you found that video?" The faintest hint of blush colored the tops of his ears, and I couldn't help but tease him all the more.

"Shut up. I was doing math homework and found it. And this isn't a nice way to treat your savior. Just so you know."

I lifted both hands in an I-surrender motion and settled into the seat. "Ow, what the heck." I had hit my heel on something sticking halfway under the seat. I pulled a small UPS box out then turned it every which way trying to figure out where it came from because I'm nosey like that. "What's this?"

Jeremy glanced over and groaned. "I was trying to keep that a secret until your birthday, but you might as well open it. You know how bad I am with secrets." Flipping on his blinker, he didn't say more just turned down a side street and stopped at a red light.

"Aww, did you get me a birthday present?" Smiling, I shook the box, but nothing rattled or made noise. "It's still like two months away, you know." Pulling at a paper corner, the thing stretched and ripped in half without really doing any good. Frustrated, I reached in the glove box and grabbed the small knife Jeremy kept there.

Pulling into traffic, Jeremy hummed under his breath and shrugged. "Yeah, well, I wanted to get something you'd like, so I've been looking around. Had to get it while the getting was good."

I rolled my eyes at him and carefully opened the box. I pried off the lid and tossed a handful of white packing peanuts at him. He gave me the side-eye but didn't say anything about the mess.

Carefully removing the bubble wrap, I sat in stunned silence. A small, green hardback book sat in the box. Worn with age and with a fraying cover, I almost didn't want to touch it. Clearly, it was well-loved from the state of the binding.

"You don't like it?" The steering wheel creaked under his grip, and I was too stunned to tell him just how amazed I was with it.

I picked the book up and flipped to the first page. "Hand in hand we come, Christopher Robin and I…" Skimming the rest of the page, I was floored. "You got me a first edition Winnie-the-Pooh?" Memories of summer days spent with my grandmother slammed into me, and I had no words.

"You did say it was your favorite book." Jeremy shifted in the seat and looked uncomfortable.

I leaned over and rested my head on his shoulder. "You're literally my favorite person ever, thank you. I positively love it." Thought on summers past floated through my mind as we sat in the silence of the truck.

Jeremy hummed under his breath again and muttered a simple. "I'm glad." The rest of the drive was quiet but not that weird, I-need-to say-something-to-fill-the-void-quiet. It was an easy, nothing more needed to be said kind of thing.

It wasn't long before he pulled into the parking lot of the paintball ring. I rewrapped my book and stored it in the box and stuffed it back under the seat for safekeeping.

Jeremy held the door open for me, and we walked inside. This place was always packed, especially on the weekend. And as we made our way through the crowd, I tried my darnest to act normal in a damp shirt.

The place was loud and busy with what seemed to be nine hundred people. I saw Jeremy's teammates right away, watching one of the large TV screens where a live match was underway.

"Looks like we're not too late, wait here." Jeremy jogged off without another word through the crowd of people, and I was left standing there, feeling very out of place in a beer covered shirt.

Checking where Jeremy ran off to, I spotted him in one of the small merch stores holding up a bright pink shirt. He surveyed me before he shook his head in disapproval. I crossed both arms over my chest as he held up another shirt. This one was bright orange and had neon green long sleeves. He gave me a thumbs up. I frowned and gave him a thumbs down in reply.

Jeremy scoffed then hung the shirt back up. With a devilish grin, he hid a shirt behind his back and stepped away from the store window. Feeling a smile tug at my lips, I tightened my arms around myself and did some people watching.

Two minutes later, he was back and handed me a light purple short sleeve shirt with a paintball logo on it. I'd never wanted to hug anyone more than at that very moment. "You're the best person in this whole building." I held the shirt away from myself, not wanting to get it sticky. "Friendship increase twenty points."

Jeremey just rubbed the back of his head. "That's what friends are for. I'm going to head out and get changed for the game." He handed over some cash and instructed me to head to the viewing area once I changed and get some food. Before I could protest, he jogged off and met up with his team, who were waiting on him.

Feeling a bit bad for messing up his night, I resolved to pay him back later. The smell of chili and cheese hit me, and I realized how hungry I was. Okay, change out of gross shirt, grab a chili dog, head over to the viewing area. After that, spend the night thinking up a way to thank Jeremy for being amazing.

Chapter 13
The ping of rocks on glass.

The diner was loud. Mostly because of our table. I listened to Jeremy's friends relive the best parts of their game with such dramatic flair Kylie would be jealous of their acting skills. Rowdy and animated, they pointed out great shots taken, the total fails of the night, and seemed to take great pride in ragging on one another. They didn't care that they were all spattered with different colors of paint and sporting new bruises.

I had texted my parents earlier, letting them know who I was with, and when I'd be back. It was so much fun listening and laughing along with them. Even the older grey-haired waitress got into it, listening to them and laughing with the group.

She even called one of the guys cute, much to his dismay. He took the ragging like a man though and made a comment on how much older ladies dug him and all the game he's got. This, of course, just made our group laugh all the louder.

All things considered, I had a great time with Jeremy and his friends. They even invited me to play paintball with them sometime. Which I so wanted to do. Finally, the bill came for our milkshakes, but Jeremy snatched it up before I could even reach for it.

"Let me get that." I reached to snatch it from him, but Jeremy waved me off and gave the waitress a twenty, telling her to keep the change.

"Don't worry about it. You ready to go?" Sticking his wallet in a back pocket, we waved goodbye to his friends and headed outside.

In the truck, I buckled up and sighed.

"What's wrong, you want to stay longer?" Jeremy slid the keys in place but didn't start up right away.

"No, I need to be getting back, I just feel like I messed up your night." I glanced out the window and saw the guys still talking and laughing with the grey-haired waitress. A grin stretched over my face, and I could only imagine what was being said in there.

"Did you ever consider you made the night better?"

I leaned back on the headrest and thought about making a smart comment, but the look on his face stopped me.

Jeremey turned to face me more and let both hands fall to his lap. "You laughed with my friends and didn't take any of their crap. Better yet, you dished it back. I can't wait to see you kick butt and take names when we get you in the ring." With a grin, Jeremy started the truck and pulled out of the parking lot. "Tonight was all the more fun because you were here."

Blushing at the memory of my paintball challenge, I gave Jeremy a gentle shove. "Take me home, Kid Curry." At his confused look, I rolled my eyes in the most long-suffering kind of way. "He was a famous old west shooter. Learn your history, boy." With a burst of laughter, Jeremy turned down a side road and stopped at a red light.

"Okay, sure thing, Annie Oakley." Unable to fight a smile, I leaned back and enjoyed the ride home.

Pausing at the door, I turned back and saw Jeremy waiting for me to get into the house. I waved to him and hugged my box closer. Even from here, I could see the smile on his face. Waving again, I opened the front door and saw him put the truck into drive and head off.

"How was your night?" Mother must have heard the door because I hadn't even kicked off my shoes yet, and she was standing there asking her normal twenty questions.

She dried both hands on a dishtowel and leaned on the door jam. Short like myself, with long brown hair, just starting to grey, my mom was amazing. I knew a lot of people would say the same, but my mom takes the cake. She dealt with my dad's issues and had a smile on her face.

"Good, went to the paintball ring with Jeremy." I flipped the lock on the door and turned the light off.

"I can tell." My mother pulled at her shirt, and I realized what I was wearing.

Thinking quickly, I told her the truth. "Yeah, someone spilled a drink on me, so I had to get a new shirt. Wasn't a big deal." Okay, so that last part was a bit of a stretch, but it wasn't really a lie.

Humming under her breath, she tossed the towel over a shoulder. "Get your homework done, then?" Mom didn't miss the cringe and simply pointed to my room. "Need help come find me." Orders given, she left to finish whatever she was up to. With a sigh, I proceeded to my room and put my new book on the bed. I couldn't believe Jeremey got it for me. I gave it a long look before going into the bathroom.

I turned the bath on and let the water get hot, then tossed my gross band shirt into it and added a squirt of girly smelling shampoo. If I washed and air dried it before putting it in the hamper, maybe they would never really know what happened. Or that was my hope, at least.

Settling at my desk with some munchies, the phone pinged. A message from Garrett.

Where you at? Tapping a pencil on the desk, I felt really disappointed it took him nearly three hours to notice I was gone. Typing a quick reply, I added a see you at school and turned my phone to silent. I'd had enough of Garrett Price for today.

I tossed the phone on the bed just to get it a little farther away from me, and then I got to work knocking out some math and science. There was still time on Saturday or Sunday for everything else, so I decided to call it a night after thirty minutes or so. Shutting down the computer, I heard a ping. I listened hard, trying to figure out what it was, but only vaguely heard my parents talking down the hall.

Straightening the desk, I heard another ping come from the window. I pushed the curtain aside, fully ready to fight an assassin, but all I saw was someone standing not far from the tree waving at me.

"What are you doing here?" I hissed down at Garrett, who walked a little unsteadily closer to the house.

"You didn't answer my text, so I thought I'd come ask in person." He shoved both hands in his pockets, and I saw the blow to his ego. "You also left the party early, and I wanted to make sure you were okay."

Crossing my arms, I leaned on the windowsill and stared down at him. "A little late to be checking up on me, don't you think?" He cringed and kicked at the ground, trying to come up with an excuse, but none seemed to come to mind.

I bit my lip and huffed. "I've got homework that needs to be done. See ya at school or something." Reaching up to the close the window, Garrett stopped me with a shout.

"Look, I'm sorry. I should have known parties like that weren't your thing. And I mean, I still need some help with English class. So can we still get together, and I don't know, study or something?" Even though

I couldn't see his face properly, I could hear the hopeful, almost desperate tone in his voice.

I pretended to think about it a minute. "I work at the library on Homer Street till noon. Meet me there tomorrow if you still want to study." Without giving him time to reply, I leaned back and closed the window.

Going for my library bag, I put him out of my mind for the time being. I had to make sure everything was ready for tomorrow, plus I just didn't have the extra brain room to ponder why guys did what they did at the moment.

The blue head of my puppet, Fuzzy, poked out of my bag, and I smiled thinking about all my plans for tomorrow. Yep, it was going to be a fun day.

Chapter 14

Lost doll, lost time, lost patience.

———

I waved to the kids as they left and listened to the excited voices fade as they regaled their parents with the stories and fun things we did today. Dang, kids are so cute. As long as I can give them back, that is.

Smiling to myself, I cleaned up and gathered all the leftover supplies together. I was lucky enough to get this spot in the Children's section. Most people wouldn't believe it, but the library is a hard place to find a job.

Pushing the last brightly colored chair under the short kiddy table, I picked up some discarded uncooked pasta from the floor and tossed it back in the box for next time. Calling the place clean enough, I pulled out my phone to check the time. One missed text from Kylie, to which I replied quickly but nothing from Garrett. My chest felt a little hollow with disappointment that he flaked out on me, but I pushed the feeling aside. If he had better things to do than study, good for him. And if he failed because he flaked out on me, that would be on him too. Not giving it another thought, I grabbed my bag and headed out to the car.

The heat from the sun felt great as I walked to the car. Fall was officially here, and I was excited for everything this time of year had to bring. Cooler temperatures, hayrides, roasting marshmallows over an open fire, and all the pretty leaf colors.

Tires squealed into the parking lot, and I cringed at the assault on my ears. Garrett's large white truck pulled into a spot taking up two spaces. Throwing the door open, Garrett nearly fell out of the truck but righted himself before taking a full face plant. He seemed half asleep as he rushed over. I did my darnest not to acknowledge him.

Marching across the parking lot, I tried not to seem like I was rushing or walking faster than normal, even when I really was. Fishing the keys from my pocket, I unlocked the back door and tossed my bag inside, then shut the door with a little too much force.

"Hey, sorry I'm late. Traffic was a nightmare." Garrett ran a hand through his hair, which didn't help to tame the mess. If looking like you just rolled out of bed was a legit look, Garrett would have it mastered. Light blue wrinkled shirt and what I'm guessing are the same jeans from yesterday completed the look.

Before I could lay into him about how I valued my time, someone yelled my name. Anna, one of the girls that came to Saturday storytime, broke away from her mother's side and ran toward me in tears. Her mother looked at the end of her rope as she fought to get her youngest son in his car seat.

Anna hit me at a dead run, and I had to take a step back to keep from falling. Babbling and crying, I couldn't understand her right off. "Take a second and breathe." I wiped her face with the bottom of my shirt, and I finally got her to calm down. "Now, tell me what's wrong."

"I can't find Sara." Tears welled in her eyes again and had to do I some quick talking to calm her back down before a full meltdown took over. I waved to her mother that I had things under control and pointed to the library. With a look of gratitude from a mother clearly near her breaking point, I took Anna's hand, and we headed back inside to search for her missing doll.

"Do you remember when you last saw her?" We walked slowly back to the library and straight for the front desk to speak with Nancy, she should be off her lunch break by now. She loved working the front desk and always wore something a little weird. Today it was a unicorn licking a rainbow t-shirt, and that got a little giggle out of Anna.

"Hey, Nancy, have you seen a doll with bright blue hair that goes by the name Sara?" Setting some books aside, Nancy tapped a pencil on her lip and looked under the desk.

"No one's turned in any dolls today." Nancy gave Anna a rainbow sticker and promised to keep an eye out for any doll named Sara.

Assuring Anna we weren't going to give up so soon, we made our way back to the kid side of the library. I started the search by pulling out chairs and looking under tables. It didn't take long to find the missing doll over by the beanbag chairs. With owner and doll reunited, we headed back outside to her waiting mother.

We both hopped off the last step, and I raced Anna to the car then helped her into the car seat. "Thanks for the help, Paisley." Anna's mother sat behind the wheel, waiting for us to get back, looking a little frazzled.

"Not a problem, Mrs. Davis." Shutting the door, I waved to the kids and turned to head home, but Garrett was still there leaning on the side of my car playing with his phone.

"You're really good with kids. That's sexy." With a grin, Garrett crossed both arms and just looked at me.

Unsure of how to take that, I decided to just ignore it. "I have things to do, so if you'll kindly move." Keys in hand again, I went to open the car door. But Garrett leaned on it and refused to move.

"I thought we were going to study." Seeing his confusion, I sighed and let my hand fall in defeat.

"What time did you get here?" Crossing both arms, I leaned a hip on the car and waited for his reply.

"Noon, just like you said." Mirroring me, Garrett leaned a hip on the car and had the gall to look annoyed.

"No, you got here at twelve-thirty. I was cleaning up the room, and yeah, I took my sweet time about it because you were supposed to be here at noon. But you weren't. I value my time, which you clearly don't, so if you'd kindly move, I have other things I need to be doing today." Dang, that was a mouth full, but it felt oh so good to tell him off.

Kylie would be so proud of me, standing up for myself and not letting Garrett get his way thinking just because he's hot, everything was going to be easy for him.

"You're right, I wasn't thinking, but I need some help." Rubbing the back of his neck, Garrett smiled and silently begged me to stay.

Frustration boiled for a moment, but I'd lied. There was nothing I had to do the rest of the day. Sighing, I grabbed my books from the car and started back to the library. Garrett took this as an all was forgiven and ran back to the truck for his backpack.

Garrett came up from behind, took my bag, and slung it around a free shoulder. "You won't regret helping me." With a boyish smile, Garrett jogged a few steps ahead, opened the door, and waved me through with a bow.

Funny thing was, the more time I spent with him, the less I got that feeling of butterflies tap dancing. I know everyone has faults, and you can't be perfect all the time, but I guess I thought Garrett would be more like the boys you read about or even the ones in movies people fangirl over.

I rolled my eyes at the thought and walked down a random row of books to the back and tossed the deep thoughts out my mental window. It was still too early for such deep thinking. "We can work back here, where it's a little quieter."

Garrett placed both bags on the table, and I pulled out some notebook paper. Unsure where he needed help, I figured we should just go over the whole test subject and then go back over anything he may have trouble with.

"So, at the party, I saw you talking to Wyatt." He let the comment hang there as we both unpacked bags and got things ready.

"Yeah, he was one of the only people I knew there." I grabbed a pen and started tapping it on my notebook just to give me something to do.

"So do you, I don't know, like him?" Brushing some hair from his eye's Garrett leveled me with a searching stare.

"He's a nice guy, I guess. But I'm not interested in him if that's what you're asking." Feeling a bit uncomfortable with where this conversation was going, I jumped into the homework Mister Cook gave us.

We worked on it for a while before a young boy asked me for help finding a book. I should have brought another shirt to change into so I wouldn't be wearing the library logo, but Garrett didn't seem to mind the interruption.

"Do what you got to do." That was all he said, so I left him there playing on his phone. Trying not to feel annoyed with him and his lack of interest in studying, I helped the kid find his books. And maybe, just maybe I took my sweet time doing it.

Chapter 15
Garrett

I said it before, and I'll say it again, she's good with kids. No, not simply good, she was great with them. As Paisley helped the kid on the computer and showed him where to find some book, she didn't get frustrated even once as he talked non-stop about his dog and new sister and whatever else crossed his mind. I realized then that she was going to make a great librarian.

Not just someone who filled the spot and told people to shush like I'd joked about before. She was someone who cared about books, helping people, and worked to educate people about stuff. Paisley was born to this. She had found her thing, and that odd hatred I had for her bubbled up again so quickly it was almost scary.

Shaking it off, I pulled out my phone, snapped a quick picture of them both then open my SocialCircle. Posting the pic, I tried to think of a catchy thing to say. I mean, this is what boyfriends do, right? They want to show off how great their girl is, right? And my girl is the best.

I posted a generic caption I'd read off some other posts I'd seen before, then put my phone away before she got back to the table. Rubbing my chest to try and release the tightness there, I thought about getting back to work. But my head just wasn't into it studying.

Honestly, I didn't have to be here. My grades were okay enough to play ball. I just wanted to spend some time with Paisley after I messed things up so badly last night, and what better place to be than somewhere she liked to be. Why I felt that way, I had no clue. But I did want to spend more time with her.

Funny thing, she wasn't even on my radar a few weeks ago. I'm sure I'd seen her in the hall or whatever, but I had never talked to or even had the urge to talk to her. But lately, she's all I can think about. I had lost count of the number of texts I nearly sent over the last few days. Never before had a girl held this much sway over my state of mind, but then again, I'd only ever had time for football. Father has made sure of that.

Paisley slid into her seat and started telling me about something or other. I stopped listening about an hour ago. But I nodded and pretended to listen because it made her happy. And I wanted to make her happy.

The tightness in my chest eased finally as I made some random notes in my book to at least look busy. My mind keeps turning over yesterday when Wyatt had his hands on Paisley. I wondered what he said to her. I had to have a talk with him later, let him know she's off-limits, and to back off.

Nodding at her, the tightness eased more, and I started to think a little better too. I didn't like that Wyatt was hanging with her even for a moment. He's such a player, skipping from one girl to another. And Paisley's mine, I told him that, right?

Didn't matter. I'd simply tell him again. I could even give her my football jacket so everyone at school would know too. Soon we'd be dating, and people would get the fact she's with me.

The tightness eased more, and I felt like I could breathe again. I nodded once more at whatever she was saying and started making plans to get Paisley to date me.

Chapter 16
Sunday sleepover.

———

Hobbling on my heels, I spooned more ice cream into my mouth and tried not to fall on the way back to the living room. I fought off a brain freeze and plopped back onto the couch then un-paused the movie. Sunday nights had been girls night since forever. It had been the perfect way to end the week and ready ourselves for the school days ahead.

"Your mom makes the best brownies." Kylie took a large bite of brownie topped with vanilla ice-cream and groaned. "See, see that guy right there." She pointed with the spoon at the TV and went on about her crush on some actor named Cosmo Brown. I didn't see anything special about him but to each their own.

"So, how'd your study date go?" Kylie grabbed a handful of chips and crumbled them into her ice-cream before she took another bite.

"Fine, I guess. Garrett was thirty minutes late, but he caught me at the car, and we ended up studying for a few hours." I spooned a bite of brownie from my bowl and wiggled my toes, checking out the paint job. Apparently, it was a legit thing, with the movie watching and ice cream eating, there had to be nails painted. Pink sparkle polish decorated my toes as Kylie insisted.

Snorting at my comment, Kylie scooped more ice-cream-chip combo in her mouth and talked with her mouth full. "And I bet he said something about how the traffic was so bad, blah blah blah." She put the nearly empty bowl aside and reached for some neon green polish. "He's so self-focused."

"He's not that bad." I didn't know why I felt the need to defend him. I mean, I was pretty mad about the whole thing yesterday.

"You need to find a guy like Cosmo or Jeremy." I choked on a brownie bit and tried to clear my throat as Kylie painted her toes unaware or more likely not caring I could have died from her comment.

"Care to explain why I need a guy like Jeremy?" Putting my half-eaten food aside, I tested the dryness of my polish, watching Kylie from the corner of my eye.

"You two just get along so well, like think about it. You both like the same stuff, and Jeremy is easy to talk with." Being careful not to smear her nails, Kylie grabbed a chip and munched while I thought about what she said.

"Yeah, I guess, but we're more friends than anything. Don't you think trying for more would just mess up what we have now? Not that I'm thinking of dating him or anything." I picked at my melty ice-cream brownie mess and looked at Kylie from under my lashes.

"Nah, I mean, look at your parents. Didn't you say they were friends long before they started dating? And look at them now. You should be friends with the person you date, don't you think?" Finished with her toes, Kylie started painting her fingernails a bright purple.

I watched the people on the TV dance and sing in the rain. She was right. Looking at my parents, you could tell they were friends. They told each other everything. I could never get away with anything as a kid. Not only that, but they spent time together. Sure they had their own things, but they always made time for each other.

And then there was Jeremy. We've known each other for years and texted or talked once a day, at least. Aside from Kylie, he knows just about everything about me. But is this a door I really want to open?

"Don't over-analyze it. I didn't mean you should date Jeremy per se, just someone like him." Capping the polish, Kylie had painted each nail a different color of the rainbow and was now adding some a holo top-coat.

"Maybe. I don't think Garrett's that into me anyway." Munching on another chip, Kylie started laughing. "Care to share what you think is so funny?"

After another moment of laughter, Kylie grabbed a chip and gave me a look. "You clearly haven't been on your social page lately, have you?" Without waiting for an answer, Kylie grabbed our bowls and hobbled to the kitchen.

Pausing the movie, I grabbed the bag of chips and followed her. "What's that supposed to mean?" Finding the chip clip thingy, I sealed the bag, then tossed them on the counter.

After dumping out the uneaten ice cream in the sink, Kylie put everything in the dishwasher. "Come on, and I'll show you." Hobbling into my dad's office, Kylie squatted in front of the computer and started typing.

I pulled one of the over-stuffed chairs for her to sit in and leaned in to watch as she logged into SocialCircle. She scrolled through her page, stopping to comment here and there. I wanted to tell her to hurry up, but I knew well enough she'd just slow down and take her sweet time if I did. So I mentally told her to speed things up and bounced in my imaginary chair.

She didn't have to point out the post. I knew which one it was immediately. I stood by the boy from the library who needed help finding a book about dogs. Garrett had taken a really good picture of me. But it was the caption that people were talking about.

Spending time studying with my girl.

With over thirty comments and a hundred likes, I felt a panic attack coming on. Everyone in school would have seen this by now. Falling on my butt, I sat there and tried to think about what to do.

"Isn't that what you wanted. To be popular and all that." Kylie said with a sarcastic lilt in her voice. She scrolled through the comments reading some of the nice ones out loud to me as I sat there and fought off a small panic attack.

"Yeah, I guess. It's just, he's not like I'd thought he would be. You know?" I wasn't sure how to feel about what Garrett posted. It wasn't like we're even a thing yet. It was one study date. Which he was late for. Kylie logged out and moved the chair back where it belonged by the wall.

"Most people aren't what we first think them to be." Kylie pulled me up, and we went back to the living room. "Look, I know some of these people from drama class, and they're nice. No one but Emily is going to freak over this. Try not to stress over it, okay?"

I made a non-committal grunt, and we went back to watching the last of the movie in silence. But this unnerving feeling lingered, that tomorrow was going to be a really sucky day.

Chapter 17
It's Monday, what could go wrong?

Dreading the day ahead seemed to be a waste of time. When I got to school, no one questioned the fact Garrett said we were a thing. In fact, no one seemed to care other than Emily. She'd given me the cold shoulder throughout the morning, not that I was complaining.

I hadn't seen Garrett yet thankfully. I wasn't sure how to bring the whole picture dating thing up to him. Wyatt had asked if we were dating, and I wasn't sure how to answer him. My head said one thing, but the internet said another and who were we to argue with the internet.

Opening my gym locker, I tossed sweaty clothes inside my gym bag and slipped on my flip flops. Most people thought because I was a bookish library person, I wasn't athletic, and they'd be wrong. Gym was my second favorite class, if you can call running around a class.

The locker room was noisy with people talking about who's going and doing over this last weekend, homework, and issues with their parents, just everyday normal boring stuff. I mostly tuned everyone out, thinking about my next class and what books would be needed.

Kylie hip-bumped me as she walked by, then spun and started to walk backward. "See you later." Waving a peace sign at me, I gave her the Spock sign back and listened to her laughter disappear out the door.

The room became deathly quiet, and the hair on the back on my neck stood. I turned and saw Emily had walked in from cheer practice. I knew what everyone was thinking, and I tried not to rush, but I want-

ed out of there. This was the one and only time at school where teachers weren't present at all times, and I didn't want to get into it with her
about Garrett's post. Unfortunately, I didn't get my wish.

After throwing her things in the locker with a little too much force,
Emily stormed up to me and tried to stare me down. "I don't know how
you tricked Garrett into liking you or consider dating you. So congrats
on that, I mean you must have used some kind of magic to do it because
let's face it, you're nothing special." Putting both hands on her hip, she
paused, and I guessed she thought it added a more dramatic effect or
something but glancing around, I found people were just not impressed
by her queen bee attitude.

Taking my time, I shut the locker slowly and tried to think of the best
way to answer her without taking this to a higher level of stupidness.
Nothing came to mind right away, so I did what I normally did and
winged it.

"Look, I really don't know why Garrett posted that picture. And as far
as I know, we're not dating, so lay off." Picking up my backpack, I was
done with this conversation and just wanted to get to my next class
without any more drama. I moved around her and headed for the door,
but Emily had different ideas.

"We aren't finished talking." She grabbed my wrist, and the next few
seconds were a blur of mind-memory moves from hours spent with my
dad. I didn't think but reacted as my father taught me.

I twisted and grabbed her wrist then turned with my hips. With a swift
kick to the back of the knee, she was on the ground. Emily was now in
an armlock, and I had the situation under control. My bag falling to the
floor was the only sound in the whole room as other girls watched, not
sure what to do.

No one rushed to her aid or ran for a teacher. Everyone stood silent, waiting to see what I'd do next. Shifting my weight, I leaned down so only Emily could hear me. "Everyone is tired of your queen bee attitude. And if winning a stupid fake jeweled crown is so important to you, you can have it, because I never wanted it to begin with." Letting go of her arm, I turned and forced myself to stroll out the room leaving everyone in shocked silences.

The thought of just how much I'd screwed up kept coming back to mind, and it played on repeat as I rushed down the hallway. Any minute now, my name would be called over the intercom demanding I head to the office, and once there, they'd call my parents, and I'd be expelled for attacking another student.

Needing to get some air, I left the building and hustled down the line of cars and looked for Jeremy's truck. With a shaky breath, I found it near the back of the lot and booked it that way.

Jeremey sat on the tailgate poking at his gaming thing. Hearing the sounds of a starship exploding, I swung my bag up on the truck bed and sat beside him. The truck rocked as my weight settled, and Jeremy tossed me a halfhearted greeting and continued to shoot down star freighters.

Replaying the locker room seen over and over again, my chest tightened, and I started to panic more. The next thought slammed into me, and I started to have an internal metal down. I could lose my spot in the library program. Taking a shaky breath, tears welled up, blurring my vision as I took a gasping breath.

"Hey, what's up?" Jeremy had put his gaming thing aside and turned to face me more. "You look pale."

"I screwed up really bad." My voice shook as I told him what happened, but he just shrugged it off and handed me some old rust-colored car rag to wipe my face with.

"Don't worry about it. She won't tell because that would mean you won." With another shrug, he jumped off the tailgate. He swung his backpack over a shoulder and gave me a look. "And she was wrong about you not being special. You're amazing." Holding a hand out to me for balance, I couldn't help the eye roll at his cheesy comment.

"You're my best friend. You are legally obligated to say that." I grabbed his hand and jumped off the tailgate then reached for my bag. Jeremy simply shrugged, then shut the tailgate, and we both started back up to the school.

He pulled me to a stop before we got too far, though. "I guess a best friend would also be legally obligated to tell you about any wardrobe malfunctions, right?" Smirking, he pointed to my shirt at the small white tag. "Your shirt is inside out." Giving the tag a slight tug, he smiled, and I slapped the hand away.

I gave him an extra shove for good measure then headed for the girl's room with only a few minutes to spare before the bell rang. Hanging my backpack on the stall hook, I lifted my arms and tried to fix my shirt. About the time the shirt was over my head, the restroom door opened and banged against the wall.

"All I'm saying is you could, not that you should." Mandy's voice floated into the room, and I froze with the shirt around my elbows and arms in the air. Slowly I pulled them down, so she and whoever was with her didn't see them in the mirror.

"It's not my style." Emily's voice came closer to my stall, and if I could have double frozen in place, I would have. Daring to look between the stall door frame, I spotted Emily in front of the mirror pacing.

Mandy stood in front of the mirror and fixed her make-up, but the vexation in the movement was clear. "It's just, first Garrett and now this. I'm just saying, she's pretty enough to take the crown from you if that's what her plan is." She uncapped a bright pink lipstick and applied a thick line over her thin lips.

"And, I heard you. Now drop it." Emily's voice sent cold chills racing down my spine at her snapping tone. Burning tingles raced up my arms from keeping them held up, but I still didn't dare move.

Mandy pouted, capped her lippy, and tossed it in her bag with a huff. "Fine, if you want to lose the fall crown, that's on you. I was just trying to be a good friend and help out." She stormed out of the restroom with more sass and drama than necessary, leaving Emily standing there.

Emily let out a long sigh and pinched her eyes closed. Bobbing her head like she was counting, Emily drew herself up after a moment and marched out without even looking in the mirror once.

I waited, letting the silence grow until I knew they were gone then finished fixing my shirt. Grabbing my bag, I unlocked the door, went to the counter, and took a long look in the mirror. Dressed in a simple graphic tee, jeans, and neon green flip flops, it wasn't like I was a toad. Sure, I'm not a model, but I clean up nice enough. But still, something in the back of my mind itched.

Why would Garrett be interested now? We had been going to the same school for years. He had never looked my way before. We didn't even run in the same social circle and hardly ever had the same classes over the years come to think of it.

My phone vibrated, so I pulled it from a back pocket and found a text from none other than Garrett. *You all right?* Oh, how news traveled in school. Giving myself a second to think of a good reply, I fished out some colored lip balm just as someone entered the restroom. They stopped and stared, so I ignored them and sent a quick reply before gathering my things and hurrying to class.

I managed to get to my seat as the bell rang, and just like the girl in the restroom, everyone in the room went silent. Cautiously I glanced around the room ready for judgment in people's faces, but most of my classmates gave approving nods or a thumbs up. The teacher walked in and seemed shocked at the quiet, so he didn't waste time and jumped into the lesson before people started chatting again.

By the end of class, I had a few notes passed to me that said a variety of things about what everyone was calling Emily's de-throning. Nothing got written school-homework wise. I'd have to find notes to copy, but I felt lighter by the end of class.

The teacher finished up early and was in such a good mood he let us do our own thing, seemly pleased about walking into a quiet classroom. Most of the time, people pulled out a phone and started texting or surfed the web, but not today. Today everyone stood around my desk and wanted the details on what went down in the locker room.

But I didn't want to talk about it. Last thing I needed was the whole event getting back to the staff. Somewhere along the line of stories people were passing, it became I broke Emily's wrist, or I took her down with moves out of the movies. All I could do was inwardly laugh at how badly people wanted to believe the craziest stuff.

By the end of school, Kylie had blown my phone up with over a hundred texts, but I'd successfully avoided Emily and her band of merry friends. Now I just had to do the same thing for the rest of my school life and find a way to talk to Garrett about his post. Yeah, both things were totally doable and didn't fill me with anything like dread.

Chapter 18
The fight explained.

———

Kicking off my flip flops, I slammed the door a bit too loud but was beyond caring. I dropped my bag in one of the high-backed kitchen chairs and went for the ice cream. Hopping up on the counter, I dug in and let the ice cream melt in my mouth.

"Someone's in a mood." The wheels of my father's chair squeaked on the floor as he rolled through the kitchen, and I felt a bit bad for slamming the door.

Offering him some ice cream as an apology, I made a mental note to do better with noise levels. At his nod, I got a bowl from the cabinet then scooped some out for him, all the while feeling watched.

He reclined in his chair, and we ate without saying anything for a few minutes, but I knew the silence wouldn't last long. "Want to talk about it?" Attempting to cut a frozen cookie with the spoon, he gave up then shoved the thing in his mouth, all the while waiting for my reply.

"Not really." Licking the back of my spoon, I mentally did a review of the day and heaved a sigh. "I mean, why do people think high school is the pinnacle of their life. Like, if I'm not top dog, miss popular, or whatever, my life is over." I stabbed the carton and picked at a large brownie bit.

"Ah," He finished his share and put the bowl on the counter, crossed both arms, and gave me a long stare. "Most people live for today, June Bug. And school life is a big part of your today. But it's not your forever, and some people get that confused. So here's some wisdom from your old man." He cleared his throat and held up a hand, waiting until he had my full attention. "Screw them."

I choked on a brownie bit but coughed and finally got it down. "Great advice, Dad." Scoffing at his way of putting words so bluntly, I felt my phone buzz but ignored it in favor of talking with my dad.

"I'm being serious. If people are being petty about stupid stuff like being popular or dating the right person, then they're probably vain, and you don't need them in your life." He ran a hand through his graying hair and huffed. "Life is hard, June Bug. Don't try to make it harder by holding yourself up to a standard of what others think you should be."

Nodding, I poked at the ice cream, which had started to melt. "Yeah, okay." I took what he said to heart and nudged his wheelchair with a foot. "And you're not that old." Rolling my eyes at him for being over-dramatic about his age, I scooped up a large half-melted glob.

"Hoped that helped, June Bug. Your mother is making tacos tonight, so don't eat too much of that." He patted my knee then rolled off back to his office.

Stuffing the ice cream back in the freezer, I cleaned both spoons and bowls, then put them away to hide the evidence. Grabbing my bag, I headed to my room to work on some homework for a few hours. Not that homework got done. I made the mistake of opening my SocialCircle and was bombarded with friend requests.

I accepted about half, ignored the rest, and creeped on Liam's page for a few minutes. I was a bit impressed. He'd tagged himself at a poetry smash at some lowkey downtown coffee shop. Looking through his page, I was moved by some of his poetry.

Darkness creeps on wings of black. Ink on the page and soot in my soul. The darkness, He wins again.

FaceTime pinged and alerted me someone wanted to chat. A window popped up, wanting to know if I'd accept the invite. Knowing Kylie would spam me until I talked to her, I accepted the call.

"It's about time you talked to me. Do you know how long I've been waiting to hear what happened?" Kylie's face took up most of the phone screen and bounced in and out of focus as she walked quickly somewhere.

"It's not like I planned on being a ninja today." I shifted on my blue desk chair and picked up a pen so I'd have something to fidget with. "So, what version of the story did you get?" Nerves tickled my gut as I wondered just how many versions of the event were floating around.

"Just a sec." After the sound of a door shutting, Kylie yelled a greeting to her parents and stomped upstairs. "I'm home now, so let me get on the pc." Getting a call lost frowny face, I closed the window and tossed the phone on my bed.

Racing downstairs, I grabbed a water and some mini pretzel sticks before heading back. Hearing an incoming call, I walked a bit slower and twisted the cap open. After sitting, I accepted the call, and Kylie's face popped up in a small window.

"Oh my gosh, what took you so long? I literally just hung up on you." Before I could answer, she when off on a tangent about rude people, I knew it wasn't really about me per se, but more to the drama people who she was forced to work with. Of course, it could have something to do with her parents.

"You done?" Taking a sip of my drink, I bunched both legs under the desk and waited for her reply.

Heaving a sigh, Kylie grabbed some origami paper and started folding. "Yes, you may tell me everything now. And don't leave a thing out." I started at the beginning. Because the Mad Hatter did say it was the best place to start.

━━━━━━━━━━

"SO THAT'S IT. NOW HALF the school thinks I'm a ninja, and the other half thinks I'm a spy or something." Leaning back in the seat, I raised a foot, pushed off the desk and spun in a circle and thought about the day.

"As much as I'm into all things drama related, this isn't as bad as I first thought." Kylie numbered a paper bird, dropped it off-screen, then started on a new one.

"Thing is, she's right. I mean, why now?" Pushing off the desk again, I went for another spin and watched the room whirl by. An over-flowing bookcase, an unmade bed, and the dresser with a pile of unfolded clothes sitting on top.

"I thought this is what you wanted. Whether from Garrett getting his head out of the clouds or whatever Emily said, you could be the next popular person in school if you tried." Stopping the chair, I watched Kylie fold and number another paper bird before I spoke.

"It's just weird, I guess. After talking with my dad, all that doesn't seem so important now." The a/c kicked on with a hum, and the smell of cooked beef floated in with the cooler air.

"Oh yeah, your dad's pretty smart." Fidgeting with some paper, Kylie made a huge effort to not look at me, which set my inner alarm bells ringing.

"What did you do?" Squinting my eyes at her, I scooted closer to the desk and leaned into the screen. "I swear Kylie if you even think about adding anything to those rumors..."

"Why would you ever think anything like that?" Folding a bird slowly, Kylie still hadn't looked at me, and warning bells turned into flashing lights, tornado sirens, and a robot lady calmly repeating the word warning, warning, warning.

"Spill it. Rip the bandage off fast and just get it over with." I leaned back and crossed both arms fully prepared to wait her out.

"I may have texted your mom accidentally asking about the fight." Wincing at her admission, Kylie rambled on quickly. "I hit the wrong button, and my fingers were flying so fast I didn't see who it was until it was sent, and I'm so, so sorry." Kylie slumped back in her pink fuzzy desk chair and looked utterly sorry for herself.

Hiding my face behind both hands, I groaned for what seemed like a full minute. This was not good on so many levels. Hearing my name called for dinner felt more like a hanging man being called to the gallows.

"Let me know how it goes." With quiet voice and an apologetic look, Kylie signed off, leaving me alone to face the parents. If mother knew, it wouldn't be long before dad did.

Striding into the kitchen, both parents were chatting, so I grabbed a bowl of lettuce and walked into the dining room without stopping to say a thing. Dad rolled in a moment later with plates, napkins, and shredded cheese balanced precariously on his lap.

"I told you I could get that." Mom walked in carrying steaming tortillas and put them on the table a little closer where dad would park.

"No need to make a second trip Doll Face." Using the nickname my mother secretly loved, Dad put everything on the table and rolled into his spot without another word of protest.

To say dinner was tense was an understatement. Or maybe it was just me, and everything was in my head. But waiting for Mom to either ask about the fight or speculating if she told Dad, it was a wonder I ate anything.

Well, no, that's not true. My mother was a great cook, and her tacos were out of this world good. Reaching for my fourth, Mom pushed the plate closer and finally asked me about school.

"Want to tell me what happened today?" Using the mom-voice, I knew she wouldn't let the question slide, and I wouldn't be able to redirect her to something else easily. My only real option was to tell her the truth and hope she didn't go to the school and make a scene.

"It really wasn't a big deal." Setting a few jalapenos on the side of my plate gave me a moment more to think of just how much to tell them.

"Something happened at school?" Taco halfway to his mouth, Dad set it back on his plate all but forgotten, then passed a look from mom to me. I could clearly see the wheels moving now, and that wasn't a good thing.

"Like I said, it's not that big deal, none of the teachers or principal were even involved." Sitting up straighter in the chair, I took a sip from my cup and wished they would let it go. It's not like I really hurt her anyway.

"That's not what I asked, and the fact your teachers and principal don't know makes it worse." Mom pushed her plate aside, leaned in, and gave me that no-nonsense look all parents seemed to have.

"I'd also like to know what happened." Leaning back in his chair, my father, a man of few words, waited for my reply.

Sighing, I told them about the post from Garrett and how Emily wasn't my biggest fan. I left the party and beer pong out, but guilt gnawed at me for the non-lie.

"So let me get this straight, a guy posted a picture of you, and this other girl got upset?" Nodding at the simplified version, I also added in half the school gossip for good measure. Explaining how I was only helping him with homework, and that was it.

Dad slapped the table then doubled over in laughter, much to the displeasure of my mother. "Jaxon, this is no laughing matter." Mom's shrill voice cut through his laughter, but it didn't fully stop him. She stacked plates, stood, and glared at my father before taking them to the kitchen.

"I think it's great. You used a wrist lock?" Grilling me on the self-defense move used, I felt a bit proud of myself.

At that moment, I realized something. One, I shouldn't take any lip from people like Emily, or anyone for that matter. And two, I really didn't care what anyone had to say about me anymore. I talked to Dad for a few more minutes about it, then helped Mom clear the table of dishes and get dessert.

"I don't like this, Paisley," Setting both hands on the counter, mom looked troubled. "I think I'm going to call the school tomorrow and have a little chat with them about it." Shaking her head, she rushed around getting bowls and some spoons. "I know how these things escalate. Watch yourself, you understand me?" She looked at me from under her lashes, stressed over this whole thing.

"Yeah, Mom, I know. But I don't think she'll do anything more." Grabbing the ice cream from the freezer, I put it on the counter and placed a hand over hers. "I can take care of myself. Dad made sure of that." With a small smile to lighten the mood, I pushed the carton to her. "Better hurry before it all melts."

Mom rolled her eyes then pried the top off, only to level me with a look. "Care to explain why this is half gone?"

"Ice cream gremlins?" I tried for my most innocent look but knew she wasn't fooled. With an un-ladylike snort, she scooped some into the bowl and instructed me to deliver it to my father.

All in all, I guess it wasn't so bad that my parents knew. They had some good points, but I really didn't think Emily was the kind of person to get revenge and try to hurt me. She's more of an embarrass-me-in-to-moving-to-a-new-school kind of person. But I'd deal with anything from her when it got here. If she ever decided to do something, that is.

Chapter 19
But magic isn't really real.

———

Walking to school on days Kylie had to get there early sucked. But I wasn't going to give up an extra hour of sleep as much as I loved her, so today I walked alone. I picked a daisy without thought and started picking the petals off. "He loves me." Letting the little petal float away, I picked another. "He loves me not." I hopped off the sidewalk and hurried across the street. My flip flops slapped the bottom of my feet as I made a small detour and headed into a coffee shop for some much needed caffeine.

I plucked flower petals absent-mindedly ending with, he loves me. Rolling my eyes at the early morning wistfulness, I tossed the stem away and walked into The First Cup Coffee Shop. I adjusted my backpack and inhaled the amazing aroma of coffee and felt just a little bit more awake.

"You addicted to coffee, too?" Turning, I saw Liam behind me and smiled.

"I think the word addicted is a bit strong, but I am a nicer person after I've had a cup." Liam laughed in a friendly way, and we both moved up in line.

"Understand that. So, would it be totally rude to ask if you and Garrett a thing now?" He stood there, hands in his pockets and gave off that intimidating I-can-beat-the-mess-out-of-you vibe. But his warm brown eyes and quick smile helped smooth out that hard edge. Plus, the fact I knew he could write some earthmoving, emotional poetry gave him big softie points.

I moved up another space and changed the subject without answering because I wasn't sure of the answer myself. "I saw some of your poetry last night. You're really good." We ordered our drinks, and I noticed Liam's neck redden slightly.

"Thanks, I, uh, like to play with words, and you know, make people feel something with them." He rubbed his neck and seemed to look everywhere but at me. So I gave him a minute and watched the blonde lady behind the counter making coffee for all the grumpy people.

I reached for my wallet to pay the lady, but Liam swiped a card before I could.

"You didn't have to do that." Putting a few dollars in the tip jar, I smiled at the cashier and gave Liam a look.

"Don't worry about it, here." He handed me a warm cup and took his own with a nod of thanks to the barista. "Come on; we're going to be late if we don't hurry." Liam walked ahead and held the door open for me. A dude dressed in a business suit rushed in without looking at us, and I rolled my eyes at how some people can be without their coffee.

"Garrett said something about you going for a librarian degree or whatever." Adjusting his backpack, Liam sipped his coffee and gave me his full attention.

"Yeah, more precisely, the kid's side of the library. I love working with them." I took a cautious sip and almost wished I'd brought a coat. Thankfully, the school came into view, and I lengthened my stride to get into the building sooner.

"Yeah, I saw the picture on SocialCircle. That's cool, though. I still don't know what I want to do after school." Liam finished his coffee, smashed the cup, and tossed it into the trash can by the front steps.

"Not everyone is lucky enough to figure out what they want to be when they were ten." Chugging the last of my coffee, I felt the burn, but it wasn't too hot to do damage.

"Wow, looks like I'm far behind the game then." Liam laughed, but it seemed strained. I put a hand on his shoulder and pulled him to a stop before we headed up the stairs then dropped some of my father's wisdom.

"Don't compare yourself to others. One day you're going to wake up and just know what you're supposed to do, whatever it is. So, don't stress it, okay?"

Clearly uncomfortable with where our chat had gone, Liam rubbed the back of his neck then changed the subject. "Uh, do you know why people are staring at us?"

Sure enough, everyone appeared to be watching us. Some were rushing around the side of the building, but others stood in groups and stared. I dropped my hand and adjusted my backpack uncomfortable with all the eyes on us.

Nancy yelled my name as she ran toward us with a look of panic. "Don't you ever answer your phone?" Taking a gasping breath, she pulled me the direction she'd come from leaving Liam to follow after us.

"Garrett and Jeremy are on the south field now, and Garrett looks pissed. You need to do something." Winded, Nancy wheezed, and I felt a twinge of worry for her.

"Wait, hold up a sec. What happened?" She didn't stop or even slow down, in fact, she went from a jog to a flat out run. Hearing her gasp for breath, it wasn't just Jeremy I was worried about now. "Maybe you should sit down." I tugged her to a stop and led her to a bench under a tree and tried to get her to calm down and breathe normally again.

Liam leaned on the back of the bench and looked concerned at the rhythm of Nancy's breathing. "Did anyone try and break them up yet?" More people rushed to the south side wanting to see a fight.

"No, some of the football team is there, but I don't think they're interested in breaking it up." Nancy took a deep breath, and with a hand over her heart seemed to be calming down.

After a moment, her breathing was a little more normal, and I let out my own sigh of relief. "Okay, calmly and the keyword there is calmly, tell me what's going on."

I heard the crowd yelling, and I couldn't stand it anymore. "Liam, can you stay with Nancy, please?" Without waiting for his reply, I grabbed my bag and ran toward the sound of raised voices.

I pushed my way through the people who were shouting for a real fight. I shoved through just in time to see Garrett shove Jeremey in the chest and yell something about not messing with his girl again. The anger on Garrett's face at that moment was nothing to the heated ire I felt building inside me.

Rushing over to Jeremy, I flung my bag, and it hit Garrett square center, knocking him back a step. With a nasty glare at him, I tried to help Jeremy stand, but he couldn't seem to get a lung full of air. People gathered around to see more of the show, but that's when a teacher arrived, and most people seemed to think it was best to make themselves scarce.

"What's going on here?" The balding man took a few huffing breaths, and the green school shirt stretched tightly over his gut. The sports coach had arrived, not that it did much good. Clearly, the only reason he came over was the fact the football team could get in trouble, and that may lead to someone getting suspended, and that would be bad for his job.

With a few words to Garrett and a look at Jeremy, the coach just shook his head and made a call for the nurse to come get my wheezy friend.

"Just breathe, okay. The nurse is on the way." Rubbing circles on Jeremy's back, I glared at the coach and wished whatever hair was left up there caught on fire and burned away. I was about to say something to him when Garrett came up and tried to pull me away.

"Leave him; we're going to be late for class."

I snapped my arm back and gave him my best death glare. "You go ahead. I'm going to stay with Jeremy." He hesitated, and I could tell he was angry. But I didn't care what he felt like at the moment. Taking my bag back, I gave him another glare. "I'm staying."

Nancy showed up and whispered to text her later. I made a mental note to check on her. I didn't like the way she was still out of breath. The coach said something to Garrett and headed inside himself, leaving us waiting. Awesome.

Thankfully, Garrett didn't say anything in those few minutes while we waited. It wasn't too long before the nurse came, and we got Jeremey to her office. I stood in the hallway just outside her door, waiting for an update.

"So, you aren't going to deny you were spending time with that guy?" Mirroring my stance, Garrett crossed both arms and glared at me.

"I don't know what your problem is. Jeremy is my friend. I hang out with him. If you have an issue with that, you should have talked to me. Not that it would have changed anything because I'm not going to drop my friends for you." A water fountain kicked on. The low hum could be heard along with the quiet mutterings of teachers behind closed doors.

"It had nothing to do with you two hanging out, not really. Look, baby," Stepping closer Garrett put both hands on my shoulders and gave me a small squeeze. "I don't want to lose my girl to anyone. I guess I lost my head there when I learned he picked you up at the party." He leaned in and kissed my forehead then smiled like everything was fine. Taking my hand, he tried to pull me to class, but I wasn't moving. Saying you were sorry didn't magically fix this situation and, did he really just kiss my forehead?

"Saying you're sorry doesn't fix this. Jeremy has asthma; he could die." Okay, that was a stretch because I had no idea what condition he was in, but still. I pulled my hand from his and backed up a step. "I'm done. Stay away from me." I jogged a few steps and hurried away from him needing some space to think. Garrett called me back but didn't chase after me. Smart guy.

I put my backpack in my locker and retraced my steps to the nurse's office. Thankfully Garrett was gone when I got there. I knocked on the nurse's door and cracked it open but didn't see anyone behind the desk.

Walking inside, I moved some hair from my eyes and searched both of the patient rooms, but the lights were out. I glanced through some of the papers on the desk for a clue, but they gave me no ideas as to where the nurse or Jeremy had gone. Deciding to text Jeremy later, I sent a quick message to Kylie. If anyone knew what was going on, it would be her.

The door opened, nearly hitting me in the face. I stepped back, but the door got my foot. Sometimes wearing flip flops wasn't a good idea.

"Oh, dear, are you all right?" The nurse was a plump woman in her late sixties with a head full of hair that screamed brown-from-a-bottle.

"Yeah, I'm fine. Do you know where they took the guy who was in here earlier?" I leaned to one side and tried not to think about my throbbing toes.

"Sorry, dear, I can't tell you anyone's medical information. Are you sure you're alright?" The nurse came in closer and looked down at my foot.

"Yeah, it's all good." I slid around her into the hall as my phone pinged. It was the longest reply from Kylie I'd ever seen, which unfortunately was more hearsay than real useful info.

"Where are you going, didn't you need something?" Hands resting on her wide hips, the nurse gave me an adult all-business look.

"I just had some bad cramps, but it's fine now." Rushing down the hall, I ignored her calling and slammed into the exit door. Pieces clicked into place with a loud snap and as stupid as it sounded, I knew this was all my fault. I just hoped this whole thing wasn't permanent, and I could undo it before it got worse.

Chapter 20
Garrett

I screwed up. That single phrase ran through my head over and over as I hurried out the door and across the parking lot. Cars and trucks sat in orderly rows waiting for school to be over. I caught my reflection in the window of a car as I passed and didn't recognize the person staring back. Walking quickly by, I tried to push the image from my head, but that phrase hammered away and wouldn't let up. I had to think of a way to fix this.

My head hurt. The panicked pressure in my chest made it hard to think, hard to breathe. I texted Paisley and waited all of two seconds before texting again. She still hadn't answered by the time I got to my truck. I slammed a fist into the side door and swore as the sound of flesh hitting metal rang throughout the quiet lot. Squatting with head in both hands, I ignored my throbbing fist and gripped the phone tight, waiting for any sound she'd texted me back.

Needing to clear my mind to think, I was up and moving before the plan was fully formed in the messed up thing I called a brain. Jumping in my truck, I didn't waste time with the seat belt, I cranked the truck and tore out of the lot heading for the only spot I knew would clear this fog from my head.

Car horns blared, tires squealed, and peopled yelled, but I passed them too quickly to hear what they said. Maybe if I went faster, the right words would come to mind and make this all better. I turned onto the dirt road, the tires lifted off the ground for a moment, and a new wave of panic flashed through me for a brief second, but the truck righted it-self and was back on all fours quickly.

I braked hard and skidded a few feet before the truck stopped sending a cloud of grass and dirt into the air. Sitting there, I took big, gasping breaths trying to calm my racing heart. I would fix this. I just needed to clear my head and think.

Throwing the door opened, I went straight for my special tree. I found it years ago on a fishing trip with father. I had hidden stuff in the hollow tree since then. Baseball cards and little treasures I'd found, just stupid kid stuff.

A few years ago, I hid a bottle of my father's strongest drink there. He never knew it was even missing. Fishing the clear bottle from the tree, I wiped the dust away and took a swig feeling the burn all the way down.

I slid down the tree and sat on the ground, settling in for a long drinking session. The phone pinged, and I rushed to answer it. *Dude, where'd you go?* Wyatt's text sent a bubble of irritation through me. I tossed the phone away before I replied with something nasty and took another drink.

This was all his fault. If he hadn't wanted to walk the long way around the school, I wouldn't have been anywhere near that girlfriend stealing geek. No... that's not true. I wanted to talk to the kid, that was it. Or was it? I just didn't know anymore.

The wind moved through the leaves, and I watched a few drift to the ground. It was always peaceful out here without all the noise of the city and school closing in on me. My phone dinged, and I briefly thought about answering it, but I just couldn't bring myself to get up yet.

The thought hit me like a runaway train. I should do something to show her how sorry I was. Words weren't going to mean anything to her. I needed to show her some grand gesture of repentance.

Scrambling for the phone, I saw another text from Wyatt waiting for me, but I ignored him and texted Paisley again. I knew what to get her, something to show just how sorry I was and show she was with me. She would love the gift I had in mind. She would love her gift, love her. Yes, I love her. I love... her.

Chapter 21
Knowing is half the battle.

———

"Why are you all evenly numbered?" I tossed yet another flower stem aside and ignored my phone, which pinged for what seemed like the hundredth time in the last hour. Taking a calming breath did nothing for my nerves as I jerked up another daisy and started counting again.

"He loves me." Plucking a petal, I let it go to drift in the wind. "He loves me not." I continued picking the waxy petals until only one was left. "He loves me." Chunking the stem aside, I admitted defeat and felt a mental breakdown coming on. Resting my head in both hands, I ran my fingers through the rust-red strands and pulled until the pinpricks of pain were nearly unbearable.

"If I knew you were going to commit a flower massacre, I would have called sooner." Kylie toed some of the petals that hadn't blown away and sipped her drink, waiting for an explanation. The wind lifted several petals as they danced on the breeze before getting flung into the gutter.

"Do you believe in magic?" Hearing my voice waver, I cleared my throat and tried to sound halfway sane. "Like one hundred percent real, not the fake sleight of hand stuff?" Sitting on the ground, I searched Kylie's face for any sign she thought I was losing it. I tried to imagine what she could be thinking when my phone dinged again.

"You know, I do. Magic is all around us if anyone cares to look for it. You going to answer that?" The phone dinged a third time, so I gave in and answered it. More cute texts from Garrett.

Hey, you get my last text?

Honey bear?

I'm really sorry about the whole Jeremy thing.

Are you there?

Honey bear?

I groaned and tossed the phone on top of my backpack, not wanting to see the thing.

"What are you groaning about?" Kylie grabbed my phone, scrolled through the texts, and doubled over laughing.

"Glad you think it's funny." I snatched the phone back and turned the stupid thing off, then stuffed it in my back pocket. That was enough of him for today.

"Honey bear, wow, what an original name." Wiping both eyes, Kylie took another sip of her green drink, then dropped her bag and sat beside me. "So, what do terrible pet names and plucking flowers to death have in common?" She picked up some petals and let them dance in the breeze.

I gave her a you're-being-stupid look, stood, and dusted my pant legs. "You know what, forget I said anything. You'll think I'm crazy anyway." Grabbing my bag, I started back to school. I'd already missed four classes, thankfully I was passing all of them, so this little field trip of failure wouldn't put me behind.

"Oh, come on. I'd never think you were crazy. At least not as crazy as me." Kylie ran to catch up with me, slid an arm around mine, then tugged me to a stop. "We still have half an hour until lunch is over. This calls for more coffee and muffins."

She tossed her cup and pulled me to the First Cup, and as she stood in line, I found a spot out of the way from anyone who'd care to listen. Claiming a small table in the back, I pulled out a chair and fell into it. There weren't many people here this time of day, which I was super glad about. Just some people in the corner with laptops and two older guys playing chess on a board near the door. Kylie weaved her way to the table after a few minutes and placed a large cup in front of me.

"Today seemed like a large coffee kind of day." Sitting across from me, Kylie checked her phone and sent a quick text before putting it away and then gave me her full attention. "Okay, we have tee minus twenty minutes left, spill your guts." She cut a chocolate muffin in half with a plastic knife, and I felt something inside me loosen, knowing she was here for me.

The heat from the cup soak through the paper and warmed my hands. "I don't even know where to start." Taking a sip, I let the bitter taste of coffee warm me as I tried to get all my thoughts in order.

Shifting in the seat, Kylie licked the whipped cream from the top of her cup as I ate my half of the muffin. "I've found the best place to start is at the beginning. But that's just me." Drinking her fake coffee with whipped cream and rainbow sprinkles, Kylie seemed pleased with her smart answer until she saw my glare. She muttered an apology, but I ignored it and jumped into the mess of my story.

"I guess it started last week." Telling her about the first flower and my now silly wish wasn't as hard as I thought it would be. There was no stopping me to ask questions or any smart comments made. She just listened like a true friend, and I couldn't have been more thankful for her.

"Okay, just so I've got this right. You wished on a flower that Garrett loved you, and now he's head over heels for you?" Slurping the last of her fake coffee, Kylie pushed the cup aside, folded both hands in front of herself, and waited for my response.

I snapped the lid back onto my cup, picked up Kylie's, and chucked both cups along with the remnants of the muffin wrapper. "Yeah, that's it." With nothing more to say, I rubbed my eyes and felt more tired than I'd have in a long time. The mental alarm clock in my head started beeping. I checked the wall clock and saw our time was up, and we should get back to school soon.

"Okay, one, I totally believe you." Even though I figured she would, it was nice to hear someone believed I wasn't crazy. But then again, Kylie's always had a thing for the unexplained and mythical kind of stuff. "And two, you shouldn't have gone with Garrett without telling your parents. I mean that's safety one-oh-one." With the use of her mom-voice, I knew she meant business. And she was right.

This I knew, of course. I'd felt guilty about it for a while now. Especially since I ended up stranded in the upstairs bathroom. I didn't know what I would have done if Jeremy hadn't bailed me out.

"You're right. I just wanted to have that normal high school date with the popular guy, you know?" Kylie checked her phone, stood, and slung her backpack over a shoulder.

"I get that. But normal is highly overrated." She fluffed out her bright pink hair and rested a hand on her hip. "And, if we're going to find some answers, we need to get going." She flashed me the peace sign, and I rolled my eyes.

"And where do you think we can find an answer to if you wished upon a flower?" Grabbing my backpack, I followed as she weaved through the crowd of people.

"To the library!" Shouting out her plan a little too loud, people stared, but Kylie grabbed my arm and made a beeline for the door.

"Must you?" Out on the sidewalk, Kylie started skipping jostling me with every step. The wind had picked up some leaves, and a few flower petals floated our way reminding me of why I was here to begin with.

"You love my crazy ways. Don't deny it." With an eye roll, I stuck my tongue out at her. I wasn't going to tell her just how thankful I was for her.

"Have you heard anything about Jeremy?" After pulling my cell from a back pocket, I turned it on and found ten more texts from Garrett.

"Nice subject change. They took him to the hospital. He's going to be out the rest of the day." At the library, Kylie pulled the door open and switched her phone on silent like a good library goer and then quickly took a selfie.

I ignored the texts and switched my phone to silent also because, library. Skipping the selfie part, I slid the phone away as we snuck passed the librarian reading a book with a half-naked man on the cover.

We went to the back for more privacy and found one of the computers on the library network. "So, what are we looking for?" Dropping my bag on the floor, I brought up a search engine and tried to think of the best way to word the search.

Kylie sat beside me and pulled the keyboard toward her. "Let's just try a general search first and weed it down from there. Grab some paper, and let's knock a bunch of the searching out."

"That's the most logical thing I've heard you say in a while." I poked her in the arm and pulled a notebook from my bag.

"Gracias, amiga. I have my moments." Kylie winked at me and started clicking on websites, all business now.

After a few minutes of searching, Kylie walked off with a list of titles and shelf numbers, leaving me to search the net. The only thing I found were fandom sites, stupid what your favorite flower says about you quizzes, and lame date night movies. "You got anything? This is a bust."

"Maybe, look at this." Kylie pushed a stack of books aside and slid an older looking book my way. White pages had turned brownish with age and, clearly on its way into the trash bin, I pulled the book closer, giving it an inspection. On the page was a black pen drawing of a daisy with only a few petals missing.

Handwritten and worn words filled the page. The phrase be careful what you wish for caught my eye. I ran a finger over the words letting that phrase sink in. I turned the page and skimmed it looking for key-words or anything else that might give me an answer.

"Where did we even get a book like this?" Flipping to the cover, I looked for a title, and then for a check out tag. There wasn't even a library stamp. In fact, there wasn't anything to give a clue where this book came from. "Where'd you find this?" I racked my brain for the last time the library bought books, but this wouldn't be something they would add to inventory. Someone could have donated it, but why would it be back here without any checkout info on it.

"It was just on one of the shelves in the back." Shrugging dismissively, Kylie pulled the book back and flipped through a few more pages.

"Well, what do you think?" I tapped a pen on the notebook, and Kylie gave me the side-eye. She hates when I fidget like that, but I had this odd feeling in my gut that time was running out, and I was getting antsy.

"Listen to this." Kylie cleared her throat and spoke slowly, adding more drama to it than necessary. "Be careful with your heart wishes. The things you wish for are not always what is needed."

"What does that even mean?"

Kylie pulled the pen from my hand and tossed it aside. With nothing left to play with, I pouted and flicked the pages in the notebook. Kylie reached in her bag and pulled out a snack cake then wiggled it at me. But I just shook my head and pulled the book to myself for a closer look.

"I know you aren't eating in the library because that be totally against the rules." Nancy rounded a shelf and leaned her butt against the table. Stuffing the whole cake in her mouth. Kylie smiled and looked like a pink-haired chipmunk.

"Normally," Kylie said around a mouth full of yellow sponge cake. "I would never, but this is an emergency, and what's the point of having privileges if you don't exploit it once in a while?" Wiping her mouth, Kylie stuffed the wrapper in her bag.

With a snort, Nancy poked at our books and raised an eyebrow at me. "Interesting reading. School project?" I exchanged a look with Kylie, and at her shrug, decided to bring Nancy in on my little problem. I mean, she knew the library better than anyone. If there's a book that can help with this, she should know about it.

So, I started to fill her in, but I didn't get far into the story before we were interrupted.

Chapter 22
A little gold necklace.

———

"Hello, librarian." Wyatt leaned on a table behind Nancy and crossed his arms. "That doesn't have as nice a ring to it as hello nurse." He seemed to muse on that for a minute as Garrett walked around the corner and knocked him in the shoulder.

"Stop messing around." Shoving him aside, Garrett grabbed the chair closest to me, swung it around, and sat with both forearms resting on the back of the chair. "I'm sorry. I was an idiot." Stunned by his apology, I wasn't sure what to say. "Let me make it up to you, I want to take you to the fall dance, and I got you this." Garrett held out a hand, and resting in his palm was a small gold heart-shaped necklace. A new sense of panic welled in my gut at the gesture. Everyone leaned in and waited to see what I'd do.

Swallowing hard, I started at the little thing. "Thanks." Yes, my answer was lame, but what else was I to say. But the only one who seemed to catch my unenthusiastic response was Kylie. Wyatt whistled low, and Nancy made a sound like she was trying to keep from shrieking like a fangirl. And I, I just sat there, not knowing how to reply.

If he'd asked me two weekends ago, I wouldn't have hesitated, but now, I knew Garrett wasn't the guy I thought he was.

"Don't say no yet. All I'm asking is you think on it." Garrett stood and fastened the necklace around my neck, then leaned low and kissed me on the top of the head. Again, two weeks ago, I would have been over the moon excited about this. But now all of this just seemed so emp-

114

ty. "I'll text you later. Let's go, Wyatt." Garrett pushed some hair away from my face and left with a hundred-watt smile.

Wyatt began to leave but turned and started walking backward with a grin. He tipped his fedora at Nancy, who just seemed confused with all the attention. It didn't stun her for long, though. Once both guys were out of earshot, she jumped up, squealing and started shaking my shoulders like a madwoman.

"Oh my gosh, this was the moment you've been waiting on. Why didn't you say yes?" Leaning back on the table with a sigh, Nancy started talking about the necklace and how sweet Garrett was for apologizing and the fact he got me something too. Instead of answering her right off, Kylie and I shared a look. I could tell she wasn't pleased by what just happened.

"Why do I feel like I'm missing something here?" Nancy frowned and crossed her arms, so I started my tale of magic again, letting her in on what I'd been dealing with the last few days. I gave the cliff note version, only facts I could prove to be at least in some way magic related.

"And just to clarify, I didn't think it would really work. Like it's just some stupid thing you do without thinking, you know?" Eyeing Kylie's cake wrapper sticking out of her bag, I wished with all things holy for something sweet and sugar-filled to recharge from my tale.

"So now you think he's in love with you, and it's a flower's fault?" Clearly, Nancy wasn't a hundred percent behind me on this, and I didn't blame her. If she told me the same thing, I don't think I'd believe her either.

"You saw him. What do you think?" Kylie had the weird book and was flipping through the pages. Most were blank, and others just made no sense.

"The quick change in personality could suggest head trauma, or he has a brain tumor." Nancy had moved into a chair and was now tapping her lower lip in deep thought.

"So, the only way anyone would like or date Paisley is if they had something whacked in the head?" Kylie snorted and shut the book with a thump.

"I said rapid change, you nitwit." Nancy pulled off her knitted cap and chucked it across the table. It fell short of reaching Kylie and flopped down onto the middle of the table. We stared at it for a moment before busting out in laughter.

After the laughter quieted down, the sound of heeled shoes from the on-duty librarian reached us, and we decided to leave before she asked what we were doing. I grabbed my bag, and after a moment, I decided to take the weird book also.

With only an hour left of the school day and Kylie off to drama class, both Nancy and I decided to skip the last class and head over to the diner. It seemed like a good place to hang out until school was over, and we could talk more about my little problem. "So, do you believe me?" Feeling a little tightness in my chest, I waited for her response.

"Yeah, as weird as it sounds. What are you going to do about it?" We stopped at the door to the diner, and the wind blew through the nearly empty parking lot stirring up a few fallen leaves.

"I guess I'm going to the dance. I mean, it's what I wanted, right?" Pulling some hair out of my face, I shifted my weight to the other foot and leaned on the wall.

"You could try ignoring him and hope he goes away." Nancy pulled both hands in her sleeves and crossed her arms. She didn't have a coat, and I was a bit concerned about it. Out of everyone I knew, she most of all, shouldn't be outside without a coat.

"That's not very mature." I watched as birds flew in a triangle across the sky, then pulled the door open and waved Nancy in trying not to look like I was rushing her. "I just don't know where it went wrong. Like, I just wanted Garrett to notice me. Now Jeremy isn't returning any texts, and I feel like I have no choice in this dance thing." Slumped in the booth, I picked at my nails and tried to set my thoughts straight.

"You always have a choice. Don't go if you don't want to." Nancy shrugged and played with a saltshaker. "You can come to my house, we'll watch movies all night or something." Abandoning the saltshaker, Nancy picked up a menu and skimmed it while humming under her breath.

"That still doesn't help with the Jeremy thing." The waitress took our order and walked off; her shoes clicking on the floor was the only sound it the quiet diner. At least no one would overhear us.

"That might be something that will have to work it's self out in its own time. Just leave it and see what happens. But don't leave it too long and lose that friendship." The waitress returned and put down two cups of hot chocolate, then left without saying anything. Nancy sipped her drink and began to poke at the marshmallow with a straw.

"Thanks for the advice, it's definitely something I'll think about. Want me to walk home with you?" I slurped my drink. The hot chocolate was amazing and left me feeling warm from the inside out.

"Nah, my dad's closing the shop early, he'll meet me here. I've got an appointment today." Nancy played with her drink and gave me a forced smile that didn't reach her eyes.

"You'll text me after, right?" I didn't want to push her on this. I knew how stressful it was for them both.

"Of course. It's not a big deal this time. Just a general checkup, something I have to do a few times a year. Really not a big deal." But still that reassuring smile she tried so hard for didn't reach her eyes.

"Ok, if you're sure." After I paid at the front counter, I decided to sit with Nancy until her father came and got her. I wasn't going to let her sit there in the quiet and think on everything that could go wrong. Not that I was much help. Neither of us knew what to say, so we sat there and made small talk.

Her father picked her up a little before three, and as I walked home, my head filled with the pros and cons of going to the dance with Garrett and how Jeremy was doing. I pulled my phone out to send off another text, but stopped dead when I saw the four missed calls from my father.

Crap, crap, crap. Smacking myself on the forehead for the loss of braining today, of course the school would call him if I missed classes. I stuffed the phone back in my pocket and headed home. There was nothing I could do about it now, best to just face the music sooner rather than later.

I shut the door quietly and kicked off my flip flops but didn't even make it three steps before my father yelled for me. Should have known Dad would hear the door shutting. Clearly, the force was not on my side today.

"You want to tell me why you skipped all your classes today?" Rolling into the hall, I could clearly see he was miffed. If it was one thing my father valued, it was getting a good education.

"I got caught up in the library and just didn't realize what time it was." I kept my face blank and tried not to squirm. I mean, that was technically true after all.

Sighing, Dad rubbed both eyes and gave me a look. "Try not to let it happen again, Bug. The school called, I didn't know where you were."

Feeling like a jerk for putting him through that, I quickly gave him a hug. "I'll try, but no promises. You know how I get around books."

"Yeah, yeah. Need any help with schoolwork?" Oh, how the guilt sank in once, I knew he believed me, and I had gotten away with it.

"Nope, they didn't give out too much. I'm going up to my room to start that now." Rushing away before he could stop me and ask more questions, I shut the door leaving me in the quiet of my room and checked my phone. Still no text from Jeremy.

I tossed my bag on the desk, flopped on the bed, and stared at the ceiling, letting my mind turn in on itself. I wished I'd never plucked that stupid flower. This wasn't what I'd thought it would be like. TV and movies had a way of making things seem great, but in real life, they weren't what you fully thought it would be like.

Not feeling up to homework, I grabbed a book from my giant stack, waiting to be read and settled in bed. Shuffling down in the fuzzy blankets and fluffy pillows, I heard a crackling noise. I pushed the blankets aside and found a half-eaten bag of Jojo fish. Sitting back, I stared at the fish. Jeremy had got me started on them. The dork liked them in his popcorn.

Feeling low, I put the bag on the nightstand and saw my new book. I hadn't found the right place on the shelf yet, so it waited there with a stack of to-read books. The book mocked me, but I ignored it and checked the phone again. Seeing a text, I unlocked it, but soon, the excitement deflated when Garrett's name flashed on the screen.

The faint sound of the front door shutting helped me decide what to do next. I abandoned the phone and headed downstairs to help mom with dinner leaving Garrett to wait.

Thankfully, Dad didn't bring up the fact I skipped most of the school day. In fact, no one had anything to say, which was fine with me. I chose to skip dessert on the grounds I still had homework, but I just wanted to check my phone again, hoping Jeremy texted.

After putting my plate in the kitchen, I rushed upstairs but only found more texts from Garrett. Mostly telling me what color shirt he was wearing to the dance so we could match colors. Ignoring him, I texted Kylie.

With nothing better to do as I waited for Kylie to reply, I checked out the closet just to see what kind of dresses I had. Mentally going through my bank account, I knew there wasn't enough money to buy a new dress that I'd end up only wearing to one dance. Because let's face it, I was more than likely, not going to any other dances anytime soon.

I picked out a few and laid them on my bed, surveying the colors and cut hoping for something a little daring, but in the back of my mind, I knew there was nothing dance-worthy in my closet. A ping from the computer sounded, so I accepted the call, and Kylie's face popped up.

'Hey, girl. How's life?" A light blue shower cap covered Kylie's hair, making a startling contrast with the bright orange face mask.

"Nice face. You heard from Jeremy yet?" I pulled the desk chair aside and dumped my backpack onto the floor. "Please tell me you heard something." Sitting down, I grabbed a pen and started to fidget.

"He's fine. They let him go home after about an hour. Doc's says he should take it easy the next day or so and to really keep an eye on his breathing. He's super bummed about it, though. Now he can't play his paintball thingy." Kylie folded a paper bird, numbered it, and set it aside before grabbing another piece of paper.

"I've texted him like nine hundred times, and I've yet to get an answer." Kicking the desk, I spun in the chair and pouted as I watched the room go by once before stopping.

"He's a bit mad, to be honest. He heard through the grapevine that you're going to the dance with Garrett. And I'm in that same boat. I'm a bit annoyed with you too." Kylie numbered another bird and poked at her phone, not meeting my eyes.

"I never agreed to go with him." Crossing both arms, I pouted and rocked back in the chair. The necklace Garrett gave me swung to the side, reminding me of everything that went down at the library.

Kylie leaned closer to her computer and poked the screen. "The dresses on the bed say you're going. Unless you're doing some really early spring cleaning that is." Sitting back in the chair after making her point, Kylie mirrored my crossed arms.

"I thought you'd be happy for me, you know I've liked him a long time." Picking at my nails, I thought about painting them again, anything to keep from thinking about this whole mess.

"Thing is you can do a whole lot better than a self-centered football jock. Let me know when you figure that out for yourself." Kylie logged off, and I was left staring at my reflection in the blank screen.

Sighing, I stood and shoved the chair under the desk, grabbed all the dresses, and started to put them away. The dark green one was fancy enough and would be fine. If Garrett didn't match, well tough.

After I put the clothes away, I fell into a mad cleaning frenzy and cleaned from top to bottom, which didn't take as long as I would have liked. With nothing else to take up my time, I decided to finally answer Garrett.

I ignored all the overly lovey-dovey texts and sent a simple, clearly written text explaining how I'd go to the dance with him. No sooner had I put the phone down than it blew up with messages back. After ten minutes of texting, I made an excuse to get off the phone then put it on silent.

Putting the phone on charge, I got ready for bed in the quiet. With nothing to keep my mind busy, I was left to think about Jeremy and how I'd planned to fix things between us.

Nothing had come to mind as I turned the covers down and crawled into bed. Spotting the red fish on the bedside table, I felt the pain of a silent phone again. Maybe he was just tired and would text me back tomorrow. Putting the fish and Jeremey aside, I turned the light off and tried to sleep.

But my mind wouldn't stop turning; my dreams were filled with flower petals floating on the breeze, of Jeremy and red Jojo fish swimming into an open book. But the most disturbing thing, the thing that made me wake at five in the morning unable to get back to sleep, was watching Garrett choking on little white petals.

Chapter 23
Everyone has three masks.

———

It was official, Jeremy was ghosting me. And if I thought walking to school by myself sucked, that was nothing compared to a whole school day without friends. Kylie had extra drama class time and was giving me the cool shoulder. Garrett and his friends were nice and hung around with me, but it wasn't the same.

Emily hadn't bothered me since the whole locker room thing, but I always had my guard up when she was around, just in case. The other girls on the cheer squad weren't so bad, in fact, they were nice, chatting with me in-between classes, but they were all very into fashion, make-up, and blah.

Sitting in one of the back booths at the diner, I half-listened to them and picked at my lunch. "Did you hear me? Hello, anyone in there?" Garrett waved a hand in front of me and snapped his fingers bringing me out of dreamland and back to the table.

"Sorry, what?" Sitting back, I noted the whole table staring and felt my face get hot at all the attention.

"I asked if you wanted to go to the football game tonight?" Garrett stared at me, waiting for a reply. He wore a tight gray shirt today, and most of the girls in school had been drooling over him.

"You should come. The game is fine and all that, but it is the after-party people really come for." Mandy said from across the table where she ate some carrot sticks.

"Hey, are you saying we're not worth watching?" Wyatt made a funny face like he was offended and leaned closer to her. "I need a hug now; my feelings are hurt." He held out both arms like he expected her to take him up on the offer.

Mandy scoffed and looked down at her nails like she was bored with him. "Your games are fun, but they would be more fun if I knew the rules." She poked him in the chest and got some of her space back, but Wyatt wasn't going to move far, it seemed.

Resting an arm over the booth, Wyatt leaned into Mandy's space and whispered loudly. "Well, maybe you and I should find some alone time, and I'll show you the rules." Some of the guys whistled, and the girls giggled. I sat watching it all, feeling unamused at their antics.

"So, you coming?" Garrett leaned in my space and blocked the others out of sight.

"Sure, sounds fun." I should have tried to sound like I wanted to go more, but my voice came out bored and annoyed. Not that Garrett or anyone else at the table noticed.

"Cool, I'm sure the girls can pick you up if you need a ride." Done with me, Garrett turned and started talking to Liam about football. Surprise, surprise. I checked my phone and decided to head back to school early.

No one seemed to notice me get up or walk away. Not that I was surprised. They were too wrapped up in their things to pay attention to anything other than themselves. Thankfully, it was a nice day for a walk and wasn't that far back to school.

I WENT TO THE LIBRARY and started looking for anything about magic flowers or wishes gone wrong we might have missed the other day. But after an hour, I was no closer to finding an answer and had a headache building at the base of my skull.

The rest of the day dragged on, one class to the next, and my head hurt all the more. I couldn't retain a thing any of the teachers said. At this rate, I'd have to ask someone for notes, and maybe if I were lucky, someone would be kind enough to share.

Back home, I quickly did my homework and a little extra to make up for today's lack of paying attention. With only an hour until someone was going to pick me up, I changed into something warm and headed downstairs.

In the kitchen, I picked up a plate and went into the dining room. "Well, don't you look nice. Got plans for tonight or something?" Dad rolled into his spot at the head of the table and locked his chair in place.

"Just going to the game with some friends. Is that okay?" The plate made a quiet clink on the wooden tabletop when I set it down.

"I don't see why not. Just keep your phone on and be home by eleven." My mother, the ever trusting one. I bet she wouldn't let me go if she knew I was going to the after-party where there was sure to be drinking.

"Of course." We ate and talked about nothing. School, work, and Dad's new project with his buddies.

I picked at my meal, not feeling terribly hungry. I saw my parents exchange a look, but both thankfully chose not to ask.

The doorbell rang right at five as promised. Giving both my parents a hug and again assuring them I'd be safe and home on time, I left in a car full of girls. They were on the lower tier of popular, hanger-ons as Mandy had told me. Not athletic enough to be a cheerleader, but their parents were still well off, and they, in turn, had money. Somehow meaning they were in the popular circle of sorts.

We got to the stadium early, but there were still nine hundred people already here. The noise was nearly overbearing; kid's ran around yelling as their parents chased after them. I was nearly taken out by a pack of ten-year-olds as they ran by with hot dogs and half-eaten cotton candy. Walking behind the other girls as they weaved through the crowd of people, I half-listened to them talking about nothing of real importance.

Stepping on a soda can, I grumbled and picked it up. "Can't people throw their trash away?" Tossing it in a nearby trash barrel, I went to find a relatively quiet place to sit. I decided not to sit with the girls I rode with in hopes of keeping what little brain cells I had left intact. If I had to listen to another conversation about liquid eyeliner versus crayon pen liner, I'd go mad.

The game was close, throughout it. I half-heartedly cheered when it seemed right and boo-ed when it looked like a bad play was called. I figured it was the right thing to do, and no one called me on it. The guys pulled out a win at the end with only two points to spare. I followed the crowd out of the stands and started searching for my ride.

"Oh, my gosh, Paisley. Where have you been?" Mandy was still in her cheerleader uniform but pulled me into a hug that knocked the breath out of me. She bounced in place, still hugging me but finally let go after a moment. "Did you see Robbi wink at me?" With a high pitch squeal, Mandy bounced away and started talking to some of the other girls there, leaving me in a what-in-the-world-was-that state.

I hung out of the outskirts of the group and listened with half an ear and watched people walk by. Parents with young kids on a sugar high, grandparents who came to watch and get out of the house.

"There you are, what did you think of the game?" Garrett wrapped an arm around my shoulders and leaned in a little too close for comfort, invading my space with his post-game funk. I pulled away and scrunched my nose at him, but he didn't get my nonverbal sign he needed to shower longer than just five minutes.

"Ladies, I have arrived." Wyatt strolled up and slung an arm around one of the girls standing with us. With a large smile like she won a prize, the girl wrapped an arm around him and twisted her fingers in his belt loop. She wasn't going to let him get away easily. "So, are we going or what?"

Everyone started talking at once and dividing up who would ride with who. "You can come with me, baby." Wyatt pulled the girl a little closer, and she giggled like a fool.

Garrett pulled me along with the others, occasionally stopping to talk to different people. Most congratulated him on the win, some gave him pointers and told him where he could do better. But he took it all in stride and was nice to everyone he talked to.

"Up ya go." Garrett had opened the door to his truck, and I climbeded inside. Quickly throwing all his gear in the back seat, he started the truck, and we were off.

"That was a good game." Lame Pays, you don't know if it was a good one or not. But Garrett didn't seem to hear the hesitation in my voice. He just took my hand, gave the back of it a kiss, then gave me that winning smile of his. The one that could make him a model for toothpaste with how bright that smile was. For once Garrett didn't turn on the radio, he drove in silence, seemly content to just hold my hand and be in the now.

By the time we got to the bonfire, the music was loud, and the alcohol flowed like water. Girls danced on truck beds in their very short shorts as some guys watched. Short skirts, high heels, and drinking didn't mix.

Sticking close to Garrett made me feel safe for the most part, but I still got some not so nice looks. Bunch of creeps undressing me with their eyes. Ugh.

With his arm around my shoulders, Garrett led me over to the cooler and grabbed a beer for himself. Popping the top, he offered it to me, but I declined. "You want something else? I think they have boxed wine somewhere." He looked around and pointed to a spot where most of the cheerleaders were passing out cups. Emily seemed to survey the scene around herself taking the whole party in at once. When she spotted me though, her face twisted into a sneer. Taking a cup from Mandy, she sauntered off and sat on a dude's lap, much to his surprise and pleasure.

"I told you, I don't drink alcohol." Getting a blank look from Garrett, he just shrugged and chugged his beer. Lovely.

"And here's the man of the hour!" Wyatt grabbed Garrett by the shoulders and pulled him into the center of a circle of trucks. They stepped up onto the back of one and stood on the tailgate so everyone could see them. "Hey, everyone, here he is," Wyatt yelled, and the crowd roared, clapped, whistled, and shouted out praise to the guy who threw the winning touchdown. Someone started to chant Garrett's names, and soon, everyone was shouting the same. Wyatt thankfully quieted them down quickly.

"The man who won tonight's game and kept Lincoln from taking a win on our turf." The crowd voiced loud displeasure at the suggestion of Lincoln winning, but Wyatt quieted them down again.

"But that didn't happen, thanks to this guy right here." Wyatt shook Garrett's shoulders, and the crowd cheered. Some guys climbed over the top of the truck with some large buckets and stood behind Garrett and Wyatt.

"Tonight's about victory over Lincoln, so here's your victory bath." Wyatt jumped over the side of the truck just as the guys dumped their buckets over Garrett.

The crowd laughed and got their phones out to take a picture of Garrett soaking wet. The girls catcalled and shouted for him to take the shirt off, which he did. I could smell the beer and the noise was getting to me, needless to say, I was done.

I pulled out my phone and checked the time. It wasn't that late yet, and the party was just really getting started. People got back to dancing, drinking, and having fun, but being here didn't give me that fun, buzzy feeling I thought it would. Don't even know why I thought it would. If I didn't like a house party, why would I like a field party?

Feeling a bit stupid, I ambled over to one of the bonfires that had only a few people standing by it. They didn't seem to be as drunk as everyone else, so sitting near them shouldn't be too bad. I wrapped both arms around myself and wiggled my toes. Flip flops may not have been the best footwear choice.

"By that face, I can clearly see you're not having a good time. To be honest, you look hangry. Here." Wyatt bumped me with a shoulder and handed me a smore. "I'm always prepared for a bonfire." With a goofy smile, he shoved a whole smore in his mouth and moaned.

"Thanks." Taking a more ladylike bite, I had to say, it was good. "I guess these kind of parties aren't my thing." Finishing the other half of my smore, I licked the sticky mess off my hands.

"Yeah, I kind of figured that much. Some of the other cheerleaders don't like this kind of thing either. You want a drink?" Before I could tell him no, he'd already walked off. Watching the crowd, I noted the way people stumped around, and their words started to slur.

"Here." Wyatt handed me a can of soda and then started making another smore. "I know about your dad. So, I get the not drinking thing, respect it actually." Wyatt's marshmallow caught fire, and he waited a moment, letting it burn before blowing it out and started assembling.

"Most people give me a weird look and think I'm being stuck up about it. But I just can't lose control, you know?" Leaning a bit closer to the fire, I tried to close off the memory of that night. Sipping my soda, I watched Wyatt making more smores. I smiled my thanks when he handed me one. This one, a little less burnt than the one from a moment ago.

"It's cool. You don't have to explain anything to me. To each their own and all that. Why don't you finish that, and I'll take you home. They're going to be out here for a while, no need for you to sit here bored." Wyatt packed up his smore kit while I finished eating, then he walked me to his truck.

All the way to his truck, I was trying to build up the nerve to ask him how much he'd had to drink. Looking around at all the drinking, my stomach sank with worry and the knowledge of the potential outcome if anyone drove home this way.

"Maybe I should drive." I chucked the half-full soda in one of the large metal trash cans as we walked by.

"I'm good, Paisley. I haven't had anything to drink other than a soda. And before you ask, everyone who comes to parties like these has a designated driver. It's a rule we don't bend on. We're not as stupid as someone people believe us to be." Opening the door for me, I got in and faced Wyatt.

"All ready, I'm glad." Lame, but I couldn't think of anything else to say.

Wyatt shut the door and jogged around to the front but stopped when Garrett waved at him from across the parking area. Gesturing for me to wait, Wyatt hurried over to see what was up.

They talked for a good minute, and things looked like they were going to get ugly when Garrett pointed at me and shoved Wyatt. Some of the other guys came over and yelling ensued.

Emily jogged over and said something to both of them, but I was too far away to clearly understand what was going on.

Whatever was said calmed them both, and Emily took Garrett over to a bonfire. Wyatt just shook his head at the whole thing and spoke to some guys before jogging back to the truck.

Feeling more than done with the night, I was glad when Wyatt finally got us on the road. Playing with the a/c and radio, we fell into a comfortable silence for most of the trip.

"Garrett's not a bad guy just because he has a beer now and again. I just feel as his friend, I should put that out there." Wyatt turned down my street, and I lowered the volume on the music.

"I'm not saying you're a bad person if you drink, I just don't see the appeal." Shifting to face him more, I pulled on the seatbelt that was now digging into my neck. "To each their own, right?"

"Yeah, sometimes it's nice to let go and not think about life stresses, to just be in the moment, you know?" Wyatt stopped once he reached the front walk and leaned over the wheel studying me.

"What does Garrett Price, the most popular guy in school have to stress about? Please." I unbuckled the seatbelt, then jumped from the truck. But before I could shut the door, Wyatt said something that brought me to a halt.

"Have you ever heard of the three masks we wear?" He held up a hand and counted with his fingers. "One we show everyone, one we show a few, and the last, we show to none." Feeling oddly put in my place, the silence had gotten awkward. Shaking his head like I'd missed something big, Wyatt let it slide. "See ya at school, huh?"

"Yeah, later." I watched Wyatt until the red taillights faded and then made my way inside. Once in my room, I put my phone on charge and totally wasn't going to stress over the fact Jeremy still hadn't gotten back to me yet. At least tomorrow was Saturday, and I had a whole free day to figure something out.

Chapter 24
Study date?

———

I drowned my pancakes in syrup. Thankfully, my mother wasn't here. She'd have a cow at the amount of sugar I was about to ingest. Dad just shook his head and stabbed a waffle wedge then pushed it through the syrup on his plate.

"So basically, I have to get a little over a passing grade, or I can't get the scholarship." I attacked the last of the pancakes with a little more force than necessary, but this was a big setback in the plan.

Dad took a sip of coffee and quietly asked the lady for the check before he ate another bite. "I'm sure you can manage, June Bug. You're a smart kid."

I slid down in the vinyl booth, and my pants made a farting noise as I pushed my plate away. "You're my dad. You're legally obligated to tell me that." I gave him an overly dramatic look that ground on my mother's nerves, but my father took in all in stride.

"I'm not obligated to say a thing. I could say you suck at the whole librarian thing, but that would be a lie." He folded both hands and waited for me to think it over as the waitress brought the check and two coffees to go, one black and one with enough sugar to rot teeth.

Watching him sign the slip of paper, I huffed. "I'm done with this subject." I flicked a hand in a dismissive wave and poked some leftover strawberries on my plate.

My father just hummed under his breath and gave me a look. "Okay, how about we discuss the guy you were talking to the other night. The one who was throwing rocks at your window." I looked up sharply, and he laughed. "I'm a trained marine, dear. Did you really think I'd miss a drunk guy on my lawn?" I drank the last of my chocolate milk, trying to stall for time.

"Look, I'm not going to tell you what to do. You're going to be an adult soon enough." He shrugged like it wasn't a big deal, and the only thing that came to mind was, it's a trap. That's wasn't the dad talk I was expecting. "Just be smart, and don't do anything you'd be embarrassed telling your mother or me about. Sound fair?" The waitress took both our plates, and I nodded to my father.

"Yeah, no worries about that." I brushed some hair aside and left it at that. Well, that was a nice father-daughter talk. I won't need another for six months. Or ever, hopefully.

My father slapped the table and smiled at me. "Good, I'm too young to be a grandpa yet." He unlocked his chair and rolled away before I could say a thing. Not that I even had words for that.

We normally went to the craft store after breakfast, but today was not a normal day. Today Dad wanted to visit his friends. We went to the florist and picked some yellow roses, and then headed to the cemetery.

The ride was quiet and a bit uncomfortable. Dad seemed to be in his own world inside his head and brooding on things.

I parked the minivan, and we both got unbuckled without a word. Carrying the flowers, I looked across the field of men and woman, and deep sadness filled me. Flags of different military branches flew high, and the lawn was kept immaculately clean.

Walking behind my dad as he rolled down the sidewalk, my flip flops were the only sound other than the snap of a flag in the wind now and then.

It didn't take long to get there. I rested the flowers on the gravestone and stood behind my father, giving him some space. I knew what he was doing. I didn't need the reminder of what driving drunk could do. But he didn't say anything, and I stood there in silence for a full five minutes before he moved on to visit his next friend.

―――――

MY PHONE WAS GOING crazy where I left it this morning. Rule one of father-daughter weekend was no phone, much to Kylie's dismay. Flopping on the bed, I grabbed the phone from the charger. I didn't get a word out before my ear filled with Kylie's high-pitched shriek.

"Oh my gosh, must you do that?" I yelled as soon as the noise level was within a reasonable zone.

"He wants to meet me. The guy from Broadway asked to meet me specifically. I can't even at this point. Like if I pinched myself, I'm sure I'd wake up." Kylie yelped, and I rolled my eyes. Rolling over to my back, I gazed at the twinkle lights on the headboard and played with my hair.

"That's great, K. How do your folks feel about it all?" I knew this whole thing was a sore spot for her parents and tried my darnest as the best friend to be there for her every time I could.

She just made a scoffing sound, and a plastic bag rustled in my ear. "Dad's out of town again, and Mom's not home from work." Her voice would sound normal to most, but I heard the disappointment there. "Grandpa Jo was super excited, though." Munching and more bag rustles came from the other side of the phone.

Before I could comment, Mom called from down the hall. Feeling bad for having to leave Kylie since she was clearly bummed, I promised to call back when I was free and hung up.

Quiet voice chatter came from down the hall, and as I turned the corner, I found Garrett talking with my mother. Dressed in jeans and a graphic tee, he stood there calmly with his backpack slung over a shoulder.

My mother's laugh brought me back to reality, and I slowly walked into the room. "Hey." Once again, lame Pays. But what was I to say? I never thought I'd ever see Garrett Price in my house.

Garrett turned to face me and smiled brightly. "Hey, yourself, ready to study?" The question caught me off guard, and I racked my brain for anything related to studying with him. "Saturday, noon." Garrett made an impatient hand gesture and seemed to wait for me to come to and remember the plan.

"Right, I don't know how I forgot that." Rubbing the back of my head, I still couldn't figure out what he was up to.

"See, I'm not the only one to forget things." His voice was teasing, but I bristled at the call back to last night when I had to tell him again how I didn't drink.

Rocking by on my heels, I turned and waved for him to follow me. "We'll be in my room if you need us." We didn't get far before my mother yelled to leave the door open. Like really, what did she think we'd do? Nope, I didn't even want to go there. I didn't listen to her, either.

Once Garrett walked through the door, I shut it and began questioning him. "We didn't have any more study times set." Okay, so that wasn't a question but still relevant statement.

For his part, Garrett didn't answer right away. He just walked around my room, poking at my things. "You still read Winnie the Pooh?" The amusement in his voice grated on me. He picked up said book from the nightstand and thumbed through it.

"What are you doing here?" I carefully took the book back and glared at him for good measure.

Garrett just shrugged, dropped his bag, and sat on my bed, falling back onto his elbows. "I wanted to spend time with you." As simple as that. No apologies for last night or anything.

I'm not sure what ground on my nerves more. Him thinking I'd be free whenever he wanted or the fact he nearly got into a fistfight with his best friend, and that was perfectly fine.

"Well, I'm busy and can't help you with your work right now." I crossed both arms, still holding the book like a shield between us.

Garrett didn't move for a moment before standing and taking a step into my space. "Are you sure that's what you want?" He ran a fingertip down my arm, and all kinds of warning alarms when off.

I took a large step to the door and flung it open. "Please leave. I have work to do." I said it quietly, so my parents didn't hear. There was no need to make a scene, not yet at least.

He stared at me for a moment gauging how serious I was, then grabbed his bag and walked away without looking back. I heard the faint click of the front door shut, and my shoulders relaxed.

Shutting my door, I flipped the lock and fell onto the bed. I stared at the ceiling and wiped a hand down my face aggressively. With a groan, I grabbed my phone and called Kylie back. She didn't answer, and my heart sank. The feeling of not knowing what the heck I was doing crawled its way up my throat, and the burn of tears gathered behind my eyes.

The phone started playing some annoying song Kylie insisted her ring tone had to be. I let it ring as I cleared my throat and answered brightly, hoping she didn't hear anything amiss.

"You called, chickadee." I rubbed both eyes and took a deep breath. "Hey, you there? You didn't butt-dial me, did you?" I laughed at the recall she had.

Butt-dial someone once and they never let you forget about it. "I'm back, so tell me about this famous Broadway guy. I'm totally here for this." Kylie's voice took on a dreamy tone, and she told me about the meeting with the big shot movie star-maker.

Chapter 25
A peaceful Sunday ruined.

―――

Sundays at my house were extra lazy days, or they should have been. Instead, I walked the mall listening to Mandy and the other girls talk about school. Ever the polite one, I tried to go with the flow and avoid bumping into the nine hundred people who also thought Sunday was the best day to walk the mall.

Honestly, the mall just wasn't my thing, but what do you say when some of the most popular girls in school stop by your house to hang out, and they find out you don't have a new dress for the dance?

So, there I was, in an overly loud place with too many kids running around without their parents, listening to Mandy prattle on with the other girls about who's dating who and why I should care. "You didn't hear a thing I said, did you?" Mandy put a hand on her hip and gave me a look, the annoyance clear in her tone.

Cringing, I turned to face her and yep, she was annoyed with me. "Sorry, I was looking at that deal." I pointed at some random store sign and was surprised it indeed was a good deal.

"Oh, that is nice, let's go." The herd of classmates moved as one to the sale with me dragging behind. Mandy led them all and walked effortlessly in her sky-high heels without looking back to see if anyone followed her. How did she walk in those things and not fall?

She and the others weaved through people like a pro while I had to stop and move with the flow of people. Following as quickly as I could, I found her and the others picking through dresses that left nothing to the imagination. You'd figure they would be cheaper with how little material they were made of, but nope, the dresses in this store were a little out of my price range even with the sale.

Picking a rack at random, I pushed the hangers aside and thought of all the other ways I could be spending my Sunday. Like reading or napping. I'd rather go to the gym with my father than be at a mall on Sunday.

"So, are you and Garrett a thing or what?" Mandy popped her gum and handed me a red sparkly dress that showed more skin than it covered.

"I really don't know. We haven't talked about it." My phone pinged, but I ignored it. If Garrett wanted to talk about yesterday or the night before, he was going to have to see me in person.

"Just asked because everyone wants to know, I don't mean to sound totally awful but, it's like you popped up right out of nowhere. You know what I mean?" Mandy held a dress to herself and looked in the mirror close by. "What do you think?" The light green dress was pretty, but the color was too pale and washed out her natural light skin tone.

"It's a nice color." I dismissed her and went back to the dresses in front of me. Apparently, the dress had to have the approval of your girlfriends, because who else would honestly tell you if the said dress matched your eyes right. They called it girl time. I wanted to call it a waste of time.

"Emily doesn't hate you, in case you were wondering. You just happen to threaten all that she's tried to build for herself. I read about it on a blog." Putting the dress back on the rack, Mandy grabbed a blue one that sparkled. "Yes or no."

"No, and what are you talking about?" Giving up on finding a dress that didn't cost an arm or leg, I turned and tried to stare a hole in Mandy's head.

"It's like this. Emily feels like she has no control of her life at home, so she has to find something else she can control, which is school. Blue is very last year." Mandy returned the dress to the rack, grabbed my hand, and pulled me from the store, leaving everyone else behind.

"If she can feel in control in school, life has order. I feel so bad for her, though." With a sad look, that even I could tell was fake, Mandy pulled me into Ultra and down a random makeup aisle.

There were way too many people in there, and I'd about had it. But I wanted to know more about whatever Mandy was talking about. Clearly, she liked being in the know, and she knew more than people gave her credit for.

"So, her parents are really strict or what?" I picked up a thing that looked like a flat paintbrush and nearly had a heart attack at the price.

"No, more like she has to be perfect. And her brother is a creep. I met him once, and I hope I never see him again." Playing with something I could only describe as a table display of different colors in little containers, Mandy pulled me over and started rubbing said colors on my neck.

Yet another thing I don't know much about. Makeup. Pulling different bottles and tubes, Mandy handed me thing after thing that I put back after looking at the price tag. I could use my stuff at home, or maybe Kylie would lend me something if I asked nicely.

"So that's it. She had it all until you showed up and took Garrett." Mandy kept trying lip colors, painting a small bit on the back of her hand as I stood there lost in thought.

I never meant to hurt anyone with that wish. It was just a harmless thing, wanting to see how the popular half lived and partied. And yeah, thinking about it now, it seemed shallow. This was nothing like I'd thought it would be.

Chapter 26
Friendship before guys.

———

"Head on up, and I'll be there in a second." I waved to my parents then headed backstage. Using the side door Kylie showed me once; I weaved through people as they warmed up and tried to get rid of pre-show nerves. Even if we weren't on the best speaking terms, I wasn't going to miss Kylie's performances.

People rushed around me doing a number of things, some quacked like ducks, and others flapped both arms and made some pretty weird sounds. No one seemed to notice I shouldn't have been back there, so I moved on before someone caught on and threw me out.

Holding the small bunch of roses, I walked back to the dressing area and tried to stay clear of the people moving props and practicing lines.

"I don't care if you have to run three miles to the nearest coffee shop, just get the man some chi tea!" Hands raised in the air and a red tint to her face, Miss Armod seemed near a mental breakdown as I crept around the scene she was making. Skirting by her, I heard a yell not to forget the almond milk, and I quickened my pace.

Waving to a stagehand I knew from English class, his acne dotted face was a clear sign of the stress he'd been under the last few days. But he took a second of his very limited time to point me to the back hallway with a strained smile.

I found Kylie wringing her hands and looking a little pale as she paced, muttering under her breath. Walking up behind her, I caught the last of her mutterings. "This is just like any other performance, no need to upchuck, you know all your lines. You're going to be fine."

"Please don't puke in that dress. It would be a total shame." Kylie spun sharply and gawked at me. It got awkward after a moment when that was all she did. Her hair had been curled in her normal brunette from birth color, and she looked super weird without the pink hair. The dress she had on was a simple, light purple bell shape, and she looked amazing. "So, stressed much?" I stretched the words out and tried to cut the awkwardness with humor, which appeared to fall flat much to my displeasure. Dread filled me at the thought I'd waited too long and lost this friendship too.

Launching herself at me with open arms, Kylie crushed the flowers and squeezed me tight. "Oh my gosh. I wasn't sure if you were coming." Anxiety and stress filled her voice, and tightness squeezed at my insides for causing her more unneeded stress.

"I haven't missed anything you've performed in, did you really think I'd start now?"

Kylie pulled back and took the slightly crushed flowers from me. Poking at the roses, she wouldn't meet my eyes. "Are we okay, like one hundred present okay?" The quiet question could barely be heard over the sound of everyone rushing around getting last minute things done.

I sighed and nodded, the tightness loosening. "Yeah, we're cool, I just wanted to wish you good luck. Or, you know, break a leg." I rocked on my heels and stuffed both hands in my jean pockets, not knowing what else to say.

Kylie laughed and hugged her flowers closer. "Remember what happened the last time you made a wish?" Kylie ducked when I tried to thump her on the head. We were good, not great, and our friendship wouldn't be like it was before, but we both decided to move past it and not lose our friendship over a guy.

I stuck my tongue out at her, and she laughed more. "I'm going to find my seat. Thank you very much." Spinning, I put my nose in the air and started walking away when Miss Armod caught me.

"Miss Paisley, pray tell what are you doing back here?" Grey hair in a frazzled mess and glasses halfway down her nose, Miss Armod was clearly stressed with a Broadway manager here.

"I was just wishing my friend good luc..." Catching the horror on her face, I caught myself and stopped before I committed a theater sin. "What I meant to say was, break a leg. I was telling her to break a leg." I rocked back on my heels, and Kylie made a funny face behind Miss Armod. I tried not to smile or crack under Kylie's oddness, which was hard.

"It's good she has a friend who would do so." Miss Armod patted my shoulder and turned to Kylie. "Oh, I remember my high school days. So young and full of passion for the arts." Hand resting on her heart Miss Armod seemed lost in thought, then grabbed Kylie by the shoulders and gazed deep into her eyes. "Don't lose your passion for the arts, my dear. It's a long road if you do." Her assistant arrived with the tea at that moment and saved us from more of Miss Armod's weirdness. They rushed off in a flurry of colorful clothes in search of the Broadway dude.

"Okay, well that's all the weirdness I can take, I'm out." I flashed Kylie a peace sign as I ambled backward.

She hugged the flowers close, and an easy smile stretched across her face. "I'll see you after the play, right?"

"Like you have to ask?" I ducked as some guys moved more props around. Kylie cringed at the near hit, but I rebounded easily and flashed an apologetic smile to the guys moving a tree.

"See you after the show." Kylie yelled, and I could see she was a whole lot more relaxed than before. Waving one last time, I carefully walked through all the people still quacking and flapping, trying to stay out of Miss Armod's view. Last thing I needed was to be sent out on a tea run because her newest assistant quit.

I found my parents easily in the front row cut-out and tried to get comfortable in the too-small chair. "Everything okay?" My father mouthed the words to me from his spot in the aisle cut out.

Lights started to dim. I gave him a thumb up and settled in the seat then turned to watch the curtain go up. Miss Armod walked onto the stage like she wasn't on the verge of a mental breakdown a few minutes ago.

She straightened her lime green fleece cardigan and stared at the audience for a moment in silence to add a more dramatic flair. "My friends, neighbors, colleagues, and hopefully, the guy I met a few nights ago at the bar." She paused, and a few people gave her a pity laugh at the joke. "It is my pleasure to present this play."

She waved behind herself at all the props and again paused. "The children have worked so hard on it, and I hope you enjoy the fruits of their labor." Miss Armod waved both arms in an overly dramatic fashion, backed off out of sight, and then singers and dancers started to fill the stage.

Chapter 27

The itty-bitty spider and a late text.

———

Kylie's scream rang throughout the house, high and fear-filled. I dropped the plate of cookies and hightailed it to my room with thoughts of all the scary movies I'd ever watched filling my head.

Running up the stairs, I missed the last steep and fell banging my knee hard. I quickly limped into the room and found Kylie standing on my desk chair, holding a water bottle in hand like she was going to attack.

Dressed in bright green pjs, Kylie made a whining noise from the chair and held the bottle closer. "I saw a spider. It was big and hairy and gross." Deflating like a balloon, I hobbled to where she pointed and moved the curtains aside. Nothing hairy or gross hid there waiting to attack us. I turned to my scaredy-cat friend and leveled her with a look. She still stood on the desk chair like some small spider could do her any harm.

"I don't see anything here. Are you sure that's what it was, not your imagination or anything?" With both hands on my hips, I tried to be patient with her, but she was being a little dramatic about the whole thing.

Kylie dropped the bottle onto the desk and stepped down then readjusted her dye cap. Bright blue hair seemed to be her thing now. "I know what I saw." She crossed both arms and gave me a look in return.

My phone pinged, and it saved me from calling Kylie out on her scaredy-catness. I hopped on the bed and grabbed my phone as Kylie

147

walked out, muttering something about dying from a mutant spider bite.

Nancy's name flashed on the screen, and it felt like a lead weight had been dropped on my shoulders. I hadn't heard from her in days, and I'd been low key worried all weekend. *I'm so sorry for not getting back to you. All is well, I swear.* That's it? I hadn't heard from her in two days, and that was all she was going to say?

I deleted my first reply and typed out a new one, then deleted that one too before sending one that didn't sound mean or hurtful. *It's cool. When you coming back to school?*

Kylie wandered back in the room with a new plate of cookies and a large bag of chips. She looked around everywhere for any sign of the spider before actually coming into the room. I couldn't help myself, call me a bad friend, but the moment was too good to pass up. I grabbed a pen lid of my nightstand and tossed it at her.

The cap hit the side of her leg lightly, she screamed and dropped the snacks. Doing a dance like some sort of ninja, she jumped on the bed then saw me laughing. Figuring out what I did, she grabbed a pillow and tried to smother me. I fended her off easily and laughed. Thankfully her attack didn't last long.

"That was so not funny." Rubbing black lines from mascara that bled down her face, Kylie laughed again, and I knew she was lying but didn't want to admit how funny it was.

My phone pinged, and it took a second to find it after our pillow fight. *Maybe next week, time for dinner so got to go.* I frowned at the message and put the phone on the nightstand.

"What's up with the face?" Kylie had retrieved the cookies and chips from the floor and bounced on the bed. She offered me one, but I passed on the chocolate and grabbed some Jojo fish.

"That was Nancy. Said she was fine and might be back at school soon. But she didn't give a real timeframe, or if she's really okay or not." I bit the fish in half and huffed. "I think somethings up, but she's not saying anything." Falling back on a pillow, I stared up at the twinkle lights and tried to think of nothing.

"I'm sure she'd tell us if something really bad was up. Try not to let it get to you. I mean, all you can do is be there when she needs ya. Which brings us to..." Without missing a beat, Kylie stood up and walked to the edge of the bed, where she toed the desk chair over.

I rolled my eyes while she hopped into the chair and rolled away with the help of the shelf and anything she could get her hands on. "What are you doing?"

"Tonight, we're going to get your beauty on." She rolled to her overnight bag, pulled it onto the chair, then rolled to the closet. She flipped the light on and picked through my makeup and other beauty things I'd collected over the years. "We need to coordinate your dress with your makeup and decide on a hairdo." She tossed a makeup pallet on the bed and glared at me. "Girl, that is two years old. Throw that expired junk away."

Instructions given, Kylie turned back to the closet. I grabbed the pallet, and couldn't help myself as I grabbed the pen cap again and tossed it at her. I skipped out of the room with a curse from Kylie. Good thing both parents were out and didn't hear what she said.

Laughing under my breath, I tossed the pallet in the trash under the sink and thought about Nancy. Running a hand through my hair, I heard the front door shut and my father's wheels squeak on the wooden floor.

"No house party, no fire, and I don't see or hear any boys. I think you raised a pretty good young lady." My father patted Mom on the butt, and I pretended my eyes were burning out of their sockets.

My mother rolled her eyes as my over dramatics and swatted at his hand. "Will you stop that, I swear." I inwardly laughed at them even as I outwardly groaned at their show of love.

"How was dinner?" I leaned on the wall and crossed both arms. Mom kicked off her shoes, and Dad rolled by muttering about the lack of a wheelchair ramp.

Kicking my flip flops aside, mother hung her purse in the hall closet. "It was fine, how's girly time with Kylie going?" At a real dramatic eye roll, mom laughed. "Surely it's not that bad." I just stared, willing her to understand how crazy Kylie can be.

Kylie's scream split the air again, and I groaned loudly. "Paisley, it's back and may have brought friends." Kylie screamed again, and I heard a thump.

"Dare I even ask?" My mother looked up at the ceiling slightly alarmed. I didn't answer but ran to the kitchen and grabbed the broom and dustpan.

I rushed passed my mother just as the second bump came, and Kylie shrieked again. "If I'm not back in five minutes, send reinforcements." My mother seemed perplexed, and I was fine with that.

Back in my room, Kylie stood on the chair, but she was now in the middle of the room. "Thank all the Greek gods, especially Loki, cause he's hot." She held a coat hanger in both hands, and I lost it and couldn't stop laughing. Her shower cap had fallen off, and she now had blue streaks on her face. "You think this is funny, look." Kylie pointed to the wall, and a daddy long leg was slowly making its way up. "We're under attack here, and the world is coming to an end. How can we sleep knowing that thing is in here?"

Without a word, I marched up to the little thing and got him to crawl on the dustpan, then I opened the window and tossed him on the tree. I locked the window for good measure. "The day is saved, thanks to me." I made a dramatic bow and smirked at Kylie.

Hopping down from the chair, she tossed the hanger into the closet and dusted her hands off. "Now that the worlds isn't coming to an end, let's talk eyebrows."

Ugh, I'd rather be dealing with spiders than anything she had in mind to do with my eyebrows.

Chapter 28

Put on your dancing shoes.

———

Garrett and the other guys rented a limo for the dance, which meant they could drink as much as they wanted and have a good time without needing a designated driver. As they passed the little flask amongst themselves, I kept waving them off, which gained me a few weird looks from some, but I blew it off and watched them act stupid.

The limo was packed with football guys and cheerleaders, all dressed to the nines in matching suits and mini dresses. Feeling self-conscious, I tugged my dress down again for the nine hundredth time. I was a bit surprised my father let me go out in something so short, but he just gave me a kiss on the cheek and glared a deadly look at Garrett; telling him over and over for me to be back no later than midnight.

Cringing at the other girl's loud laughter, I stared out the window before opening my phone and checking for a text or something from Jeremy. With a sigh, I jammed it back in my small bag and tried to think about how much fun this was going to be. After all, I'd always wanted to go to a dance with Garrett and now was my chance.

"Something wrong?" Garrett leaned into my space, and I caught the smell of booze on his breath. The smell turned my stomach. I leaned back, trying to get some space back.

"Nope, just ready to get to the party." Forcing a smile, Garrett put an arm around my shoulders and pulled me closer. Watching all the others get drunk and handsy wasn't my idea for a fun night. Thankfully, we got to the school, and I hopped out without waiting for Garrett to help me.

The other couples stumbled from the limo as I checked out what the party planning people had done. They had decked out the school with balloons and streamers in shades of blue and gold. The music was so loud I heard it from outside. At least it wasn't that stuff Garrett always seemed to listen to.

Some couples were arriving in limos like ours, while others seemed to have their parent's cars for the night. Feeling a hand slide around my waist, I tried to skirt to the side, but Garrett pulled me into his arms. "Relax, this is going to be fun." Tugging me along, we walked into the gym, and I could already tell, this was going to be a long night.

With another tug, Garrett pulled me over to talk with the rest of the football team. Back slaps and complicated handshakes were exchanged, and they started talking about sports while the girls made a beeline for the restroom to check their makeup or something. Detangling myself from him, I made my way to the food table. A haven for socially awkward people like myself.

Draining a cup of some overly sweet punch, I pulled out my phone again and checked for anything from my friends. Seeing a missed text, I opened it and was a bit forlorn. *Jeremy and I are at the paintball place if you feel like ditching the dance and having some real fun.*

"Not having a good time?" Garrett stood a few feet away, observing at me. With both hands in his jean pockets and long sleeve shirt rolled up his forearms, he looked amazing.

"I'm having a great time. I just needed something to drink." I wiggled the red plastic cup at him, and he politely refilled it for me.

Stepping close, Garrett rubbed his fingers over my bare shoulders. "I'm really glad you came with me." The feeling of going too fast clawed its way up my throat. Taking a step back, I smiled at him then stuffed a cookie in my mouth so I couldn't comment the same thing.

Inspecting the room and those around me, I wanted to blush at some of the dancing going on. One of the party chaperons I spotted by the doors was on his phone with a bored expression. Looks like the math teacher picked the short straw.

"Do you want to dance?" Garrett leaned into my space again, and the overly sweet smell of his breath turned my stomach. While he may not seem drunk, he was heading that way. I wasn't sure if I wanted to be around him when he got there.

"These heels are really hurting my feet. I think I'd like to just sit for a minute or two." Seemly disappointed, Garrett nonetheless took my hand and led me to a table where his friends sat. Pulling a seat out for me, I tugged my skirt down and sat.

I knew some people at the table by face if not by name. You had to yell to hear anything beyond the music, so I sat there with my cup and listened to broken conversations and sipped the overly sweet punch. Garrett sat beside me with a hand over the back of my chair like he was letting the whole school know I was there with him.

The girls came and went, dancing and having their kind of fun. The little flask was passed around again, and everyone took a swig. I again passed on the alcohol and sat poking at my phone.

The DJ took a break and played some canned music that was slow and sounded like love songs of some sort. That's when I noticed Emily standing near the far wall by herself.

Dressed in a gorgeous deep red dress with hair pinned up, she looked every bit of a fall fest queen. Gazing around the table, I saw no one acknowledge her standing there, and I felt a deep hollow hurt about that. Because of some stupid wish, I disrupted her life. No, I did more than that, I showed Emily that in the grand scale of things, she didn't have any real friends. Not like I had in Kylie and Jeremy. Because while I wasn't one hundred percent on talking terms with Jeremy at the moment, I would fix that.

But what did she have to fix? Everyone seemed to have dropped her without thought like it was nothing to them. If everything when back the way it was before I made that wish, would she call anyone at this table friend?

Standing, I ignored Garrett's questions and made my way over to her weaving through the crowd of people. Halfway across the room, I slowed my pace and tried to think of something to say that would fix what I've done, but nothing came to mind. I mean, what could I say, sorry I made a wish on a magical flower and took your man. Somehow I didn't think that would go over well. With nothing coming to mind, I leaned on the wall beside her and said nothing.

"Go ahead and say it." The bitter note in her voice wasn't lost on me. Emily crossed both arms and wrapped them around her middle like a shield against anything I had to say. The fact she felt the need to protect herself around me left a hollow spot in my chest.

"Your dress is really pretty. No, that's not the right word for it, more like gorgeous. That color really compliments your eyes. And your heels, I wish I had the confidence to wear something like them." Looking down at my barely-there heels, I wished I could have worn some flip flops, but Kylie nearly had a cow when I suggested it.

"That's not what... What?" Emily turned, and for the first time since we've met, seemed to really look at me. Not just what I was wearing on the outside but at my words and what I said to her.

"I'm also really sorry about your arm. I hope I didn't hurt you. My dad is a marine, and he taught me some stuff. I just reacted like he showed me." I bit my lower lip and then thought better of it. I probably had lipstick on my teeth now. Pulling down my dress again, I looked anywhere but at Emily.

"You're not what I expected." With a huff, Emily turned back to my table and watched Mandy laughing loudly, throwing her head back and making more noise than should be allowed.

"What did you expect?" Racking my mind for all the times we've talked or been in the same room, I couldn't think of any time I might have been rude or even outright mean to her.

"Most people would be glad to see me here by myself. Take Mandy, she's been waiting for me to screw up for years. Look around and see for yourself." Sweeping a hand around the room, I surveyed the people around us and caught them turning and whispering behind hands, some outright laughing.

"Well, I'm not most people," Watching her closely, I saw a flash of hurt shadow her face, but it was gone quickly. Replaced with a look of indifference, like she couldn't care less about what people said about her. But, like I told Kylie, words and actions can cut deep. I wasn't going to be a part of the party holding the knives. "Come on." Without waiting for a reply, I grabbed her hand and pulled, making a beeline for the table.

Cutting through the crowd, I saw people gawking, but I boldly stared them down until they looked away. It didn't last long though, as we passed more and more tables, I started to feel their stares hitting the back of my head, but I didn't let what people might be thinking stop me from doing what needed to be done.

I slid my chair out and pulled Emily over, making it clear she was going to sit with us, and I wasn't going to take no for an answer. Others at the table fell silent but not for long. Mandy sneered at Emily then grabbed her date's hand, making it clear she didn't want to be around the table anymore.

"Come on everyone, this is a great song let's dance for a little while." Sauntering off, Mandy seemed to put extra effort to sway her hips. How she didn't throw something out of line, I'll never know.

"You coming?" Garrett stood and held out a hand for me to join them, out of the corner of my eyes, I saw Emily try very hard not to look at us. If things had been different, he'd be asking Emily that question, not me.

"No, I don't know this song. I think Emily does, though." For the first time, Garrett seemed to notice Emily sitting by me. He gave me one last look before offering a hand to her in a silent question.

Unsure what to do, Emily looked to me. I gave her a nod and a smile to let her know I was totally fine with them dancing together. With a small smile of thanks, Emily took his hand, and they both walked off to the dance floor.

Mandy saw what happened and made an effort to dance harder. Like if she danced harder than anyone there, obviously she was having the most fun. Her date was nearly taken out by a stray elbow, and I had to cover my mouth to keep Mandy from knowing I was laughing at her.

Putting them all out of my head, I checked my phone again, but there was nothing there. A hollow feeling settled in my chest, and I fought tears. I didn't know what I thought would happen, but this cold wall from Jeremy hurt.

A plate of cookies slid across the table and would nearly have fallen in my lap if I hadn't stopped them. Wyatt was dressed to the nines with his usual fedora, and I gave him a what-the-heck look. "When I'm sad,

I like to eat." Shoving a whole cookie shaped like a snowflake in his mouth Wyatt tried to chew but seemed to have a problem with it.

Handing my cup of overly sweet punch over, he drank the whole thing in one go like it was a shot glass. Shaking like a dog, he returned the empty cup." Thanks, that was a little dry. Bet Miss Paul from home economics made them."

"Not a problem." I crossed my legs then quickly uncrossed them when the dress rose and showed way too much thigh.

Eyeing my legs, Wyatt made a comical growling noise and grabbed another cookie, this one shaped like a red Christmas stocking. "So, like I was saying before a cookie tried to kill me. I eat food, like cookies, when I'm sad or going through something. So what are you sad about?"

Pondering what to say, I watched Wyatt munch on the cookie then grabbed one for myself just to give myself extra time to put some thoughts in order.

Nibbling on the snowman's black top hat, I watched Emily dancing. By the smile, I knew she was having fun. "Mostly that thing you said about people having the three masks. I guess I'm seeing some other masks that I hadn't yet, and it's changing the way I think about some people. And I'm just not sure if I like that or not." I frowned at my now empty cup. Wyatt jumped up and got us both something to drink.

Unfortunately, before he got back, the song was over, and most everyone came back to the table. I gave Emily a smile as she sat down and grabbed a sugar cookie for herself.

The next song was a slower one, and Garrett once again tried to get me to dance, but the girl who sat next to me in English had walked over and asked him for a dance. She was so shy and awkward about it acting as if he'd already denied her. I practically shoved them both onto the dance floor.

Wyatt handed me a cup and sat down across from me. "What do you think, Emily? Are people always like you think they are?" He shoved another cookie in his mouth and leaned back in the chair, crossing his legs, trying too hard to be cool.

"No, people are more complicated than you first think. Some are one hundred present different than what you thought they were." Emily turned and stared at Mandy as she danced and laughed.

"What's the point, Wyatt?" I stared as he rolled the sleeves of the white buttondown shirt to his elbows.

"Nothing, ladies. Enemies can turn into friends, and librarians can be sexy." Making another growling noise, I jumped up and tried to snatch Wyatt's hat, but he was too quick.

Flying away from me, he nearly fell over but saved himself and, in turn, ran into a girl wearing a short green dress. "Hello lovely, like to dance?" Not giving her a choice, Wyatt turned the shocked girl in a spin and danced her over to where everyone was spinning around the dance floor before the poor girl knew what happened.

But his words left me wondering about things. Garrett wasn't who I thought he was, and yeah, that's fine, to each their own and all that. But was Kylie right about Jeremy? He couldn't like me, not anything more than just friendship anyways. I mean, I'd known him all my life. But that would explain the way he was acting. Looking at my phone again, I poked around a minute before gently tossing it on my bag.

"Waiting on a text from your nerdy boyfriend?" Emily crossed her legs and seemed unconcerned at the amount of upper thigh on show.

"He's not my boyfriend. I mean... he's a boy who's my friend, but it's not like that." I tried not to fidget under her stare, but I couldn't seem to help it. Sliding back in the chair, I looked around the room and tried not to catch her eyes.

"But you want him to be," Emily said in a sing-song voice. My body seemed to think this was the best time to go red, and heat flooded my face. "Y'all make a cute couple, and he's totally into you, by the way."

"Really!?" Cringing at the high pitch of my voice, I crossed both arms and tried for calm.

"Girl, he is so into you, why haven't you two dated or anything?" Emily uncrossed her legs and leaned closer to me like I had a great secret to tell her.

"I didn't know. After this whole thing with Garrett, though, I think we're over before we've even gotten together." I took a shuttering breath and felt a tear fall. Grabbing my bag, I stood and hurried to the restroom. Maybe I could outrun the hurt pulsing in my chest from the silent phone and unreturned texts.

Chapter 29
Cheap gold plastic.

———

I dried my eyes then looked at my reflection and scowled. Mandy was right. I should've gotten the expensive lipstick. Maybe then the color wouldn't appear all rubbed off and smeared.

Wiping my eyes again, I took out the cheap lip color and carefully reapplied the top lip. Happy with it, I started to fill the bottom lip when the door slammed onto the wall, and an angry Mandy filled the doorway.

"What do you think you're doing?" She tried for a yelling whisper but failed as her voice rang throughout the small restroom.

"I'm reapplying my lip color. Did you want some, it's a lovely color if I say so myself." I held it out for her knowing it was only going to make her even madder. But just like when I had reached this point with Emily, I decided to stand up for myself and draw the line when it came to Mandy's bad attitude.

"No, I don't want any of your cheap dollar store crap. Do you have any idea what people are talking about? You let Garrett dance with Emily, you wanted to take her down and be queen, right? Well, this isn't the way to do it." Mandy's face turned an ugly red color, and all I felt was sorry for her.

"I never said I wanted to take down Emily or be fall queen. And I don't care what people think about me. You should try it sometime." I turned and added some more color to my lips and let Mandy stew.

"You're right, who'd vote for you anyway." She sneered and looked happy about the possibility of making me upset. But she didn't get it. In fact, I didn't get it until a little bit ago.

"I'd vote for her." Emily walked into the restroom and strolled to the sink to wash her hands. Mandy seemed to pale as she realized Emily had heard part of the conversation.

"Aww, you would?" I put my cheap lipstick away and turned to Emily as she ripped a paper towel from the dispenser.

"Why not, you're nice, and you'd make a great queen." Emily smiled at me, and it was a genuine, happy thing. "Come on; voting starts soon. If you will excuse us." Emily took my hand, and we walked out of the restroom arm in arm, leaving Mandy alone to think about her life choices.

———————

BACK IN THE GYM, THE music was still a little loud, and someone from the dance committee had started handing out voting cards. Taking one for myself, I looked at who was listed.

Garrett, Neal, and Wyatt were listed on one side. Emily, Kat, and I on the other. Studying the card, I thought about the last few days, then looked around at everyone in the room. The lights and noise and how it all was really for nothing. Next year no one was going to care who was fall queen this year, who was the most popular, or the most liked person in school.

In a few short years, we'd be going separate ways and some of these people I would never see again. Not only was that an exciting thought, but it was also a scary one. Crumbling up my card, I tossed it on a table smiling. I wasn't going to play this game anymore.

Glancing around the room of people dancing, I wondered how many would think of these as the best years of their life. Something flashed to the left, and I spotted the photo area where Nancy was taking pictures.

Weaving through the crowd, I found a spot behind her where I'd be out of the way and waited for her to see me.

Couples smiled and posed, and I won't say I didn't envy them because, in a small way, I did. But I wasn't going to let that stop me from doing what I knew I needed to do.

Nancy saw me after a moment and gave me an eyebrow lift. I winced as I walked over and wrung both hands together. I should have thought about what to say.

"I'm sorry. No, let me finish." Holding up a hand to keep Nancy from interrupting, I sighed and went on. "I've been a terrible friend to you and everyone else. I've been so wrapped up in my own thing I haven't checked up on you like a real friend would have. I'm so sorry, I'm not even going to ask for your forgiveness."

Seemingly a little stunned, Nancy didn't say anything. Shoulders drooping, I sighed and resigned myself to a lost friend. But after a moment more, Nancy grinned and gave me a hug.

"That was a mouth full." Laughing, she waved the next group over and turned back to me. "I'm fine, it was just a normal yearly checkup, and everything is fine."

Relieved, I made a silent vow to be a better friend and gave Nancy another hug. "You might want to get back to it. Your line is building up." She rolled her eyes but smiled anyway. As much as she detested taking candid shots, she was a great photographer and loved every minute of it.

Emily wandered over, and Nancy gave her a tentative smile before squeezing my hand and getting back to work.

"It's been fun and all, but I got to do a thing." Picking up the dress, so I didn't fall, I hurried toward the door, but Emily gabbed an arm before I could get out of reach.

She stared at me a moment, but I didn't give her an answer. Something seemed to click for her, and she smiled. "Sure thing, but first, we have to get pictures."

Without waiting for an answer, she tugged me over to the line where all the other couples waiting for their turn. Garrett and some of the others found us not too much later, and everyone got a group picture. Some were goofy and other more serious, but it was fun. I was glad I had something to remember this night.

"You're having fun, then?" Garrett wrapped an arm around my shoulders and hugged me close.

"Yeah, it's great. Look, I've had fun, but after this, I need..." The music cut out, the mic screeched, and people groaned as a teacher tried to get everyone's attention.

"I hope everyone is having a great night. The party planning committee did an amazing job this year. How about we give them a hand?" It took a moment to get everyone quiet again so she could be heard. "Now, first things first. This year's king is, Garrett Price." Surprise surprise. People clapped, cheered, and a few guys gave him back-slapping hugs as he walked onto the stage.

Taking the moment they were crowning Garrett as my chance to leave, I weaved around people and made my escape. Or that was the plan until I heard my name called over the loudspeaker. "Miss Paisley Jones." Turning to face the stage, I stood frozen in place, not sure what to do.

Surely she didn't just say I won fall queen because that was just unfeasible.

Emily came over with an amused smile and pulled me until I was near the stage. "I can't believe I'm going to say this, especially to the one who nearly broke my arm off, but you deserve it." Pushing me the rest of the way to the stage, Emily whooped and yelled right along with the rest of them.

Stumbling onto the stage, I walked carefully over the stand next to Garrett and faced the crowd. Mentally telling myself not to upchuck, I tried to breathe and follow what Mis Mary was saying.

Miss Mary placed a crown on my head as I tried not to stare at the bright spotlight, but I felt blinded by the unexpected weight of the thing resting on my head. It was just cheap plastic, but the weight was there none the less.

Surveying everyone in the room, I saw Emily clapping, and Wyatt let out a loud wolf whistle. Mandy clapped slowly, and her smile held a smugness at Emily's loss.

"And now for the dance." Miss Mary made a hand gesture, and the DJ started playing a slow song. Garrett took my hand and pulled me down the short steps and to the dance floor. People parted like the biblical Red Sea, and then we stood in the center of the room under the hot lights.

With both hands on my hips, the music got just a bit slower, and Garrett leaned in close. Close enough, I felt his warm breath on the side of my face. "Relax, you look scared to death or something. This is supposed to be fun, chill, and let loose." Easy for him to say. He was used to everyone looking at him.

"Can I ask you a question?" Watching people from the corner of my eye, I saw some start to make their way onto the dance floor. Wyatt always the gentlemen took Emily's hand and bowed low, then he spun her around, causing her to throw her head back and laugh.

"You can ask me anything." Tightening his grip, Garrett pulled me closer, and his hand rested just a little too low for my liking.

"What's my favorite color?" He didn't fumble a step, but he did slow down and look at me.

"I don't know, pink?" Others continued to join us on the dance floor, and soon it was shoulder to shoulder.

"What about my favorite shake at the diner?" This time Garrett stopped and looked around the room before turning back to me.

"I don't know. What does it matter?" Seeing the clear frustration on his face, I let him know what had been on my mind all night.

"My favorite color is green. But not like grass green, more like hunter green. My favorite is strawberry shakes with three cherries on top. I love red Jojo fish, and I hate all donuts with the fiery heat of a thousand suns." Stepping back from Garrett, I could clearly see he didn't get where I was going with any of this. I hated to bring it up here and now of all places, but this couldn't wait, and there was no way around it.

"I'm sorry you're upset, and if I've done something that hurt you, I'm sorry, baby. I love you."

My chest felt like it was caving into itself, just a black void of hurt and things that could never be.

"But why?" The question came out pleading as I took another step back from him. I could see others had started to take note that we were just standing there when the DJ changed to a fast song. The faces turned from us, and everyone started dancing once again, everyone but us two.

"What do you mean why? I just do." Standing there watching me, Garrett seemed so much less than who I thought he was. All of this around me seemed so much less than what I held it up to be.

"I'm sorry, but I have to go." I turned and headed for the door, but Garrett pulled me to a stop and spun me around to face him.

"Don't go, baby. I'm sorry." He leaned close, and I could smell his body wash, booze, and the breath mints he thought could cover it all.

"I'm sorry. I just can't do this. Not with you." Pulling my hand from his, I tried so hard not to see the hurt on his face. Walking away, I didn't turn back. I just left him standing there in the middle of the dance floor by himself.

Rushing through the other dancers, I tried to bring up a taxi app, but I kept bumping into people. Some stared, and others told me to watch where I was going, but I rushed passed them too quick to reply. There was somewhere I needed to be and someone important I had to speak with.

"Hey, girl. Where you off to in such a hurry?" Wyatt looked a bit more clear-headed than the others who'd been passing the bottle around. Come to think of it; I didn't think I'd ever seen him drunk.

Filing that away for later thought, I pushed through a small crowd of girls swaying to the music and finally got the app opened. "I've got somewhere else I need to be." Taking off the crown, I had to detangle it leaving my hair in a fluffed up mess. Spotting our table, I cut through more people and handed the gold-painted plastic to Emily. "I've got to run, think you can take over fall queen duty for me?"

Emily smiled with a look of understanding and delight. "I can totally rock this for you. Tell Jeremy we said hi." Unable to deny where I was going, I simply waved goodbye as butterflies started tap dancing away. This was either the best idea I'd ever had or the stupidest. Either way, tonight was going to change my whole life. That thought alone made my gut turn.

Chapter 30
I'm available if you are.

The noise level was almost too loud as I rushed through the crowd. I got some weird looks in my formal dress but, one thing I had learned in the last few days was to care less about what people thought. So, I walked with my head high as I texted Jeremey again, uncaring about the younger kids who pointed and laughed.

Kylie was easy to spot with her new blue dye job. She was standing in line for mini corndogs and chatting with the guy in front of her. Waving, she caught sight of me and then pointed to the paintball pit. Turning, I weaved around trying to see through the crowd then I finally spotted him.

Jeremy was on his cell, facing the paintball pit clearly frustrated with something. I walked closer and caught the tailend of whatever was going on. "I know... I, can't you just skip it?" Jeremey waited a moment and nodded before saying he understood and hung up.

"Bad night?" Fidgeting with my dress, I waited for him to answer, feeling all kind of stupid now for not stopping at home to change first.

"You could say that. A friend bailed on me and left us one guy short. And everyone is too busy or just can't make it out here. So the team can't play." Jeremey crossed both arms and leaned back on the glass wall, unflinching as paint splatted against the glass here and there. "Nice dress, where's pretty boy?" His tone held venom, and I recoiled at the sound. Jeremy surveyed the room like he thought Garrett might jump out and punch him again for just talking to me.

169

"Still at the dance, I guess." I shrugged and pulled at the dress, studying the color, and yeah, I looked nice. To say this was awkward was an understatement. "Turns out, he wasn't the guy I thought he was, and you were right." I crossed both arms and swayed on my feet, bracing myself for what I was about to ask. "I'm available to tag in and play, if you'll have me on your team, that is."

I put the ball in his court. If he still didn't want to be friends, I would accept it with grace and not cry or show how devastated it would leave me. Just the thought that he didn't want me around anymore felt like a hole would open up in my chest.

Studying the whole room and doing everything to not look at me, his gaze finally landed on my feet. "You can't play in that kind of shoes." If a land shark had walked over and taken a meaty bite of my arm right then, it would have been less painful than the words Jeremy had half-heartedly flung at me. But what did I really expect. I'd dropped him just like Emily's friends dropped her, and I was a terrible person for it.

Inspecting my shoes, I rocked on them and cleared the large lump from my throat. "Okay, I just wanted to say I was available if you wanted me or anything. See you around school, I guess." With a small wave, I bit my lip and walked away trying so hard not to make a sound as I fought back an overwhelming wave of pain and regret. The crowd blurred, but I didn't have to see to know I'd messed up big time, and there was nothing I could do to fix this.

A hand gripped my upper arm and pulled me to a stop. "How available are you?" I blinked to cleared my vision and watched as Jeremey's face seemed to slowly turn a shade of red.

"Like, not tied down, a free agent. Ready and willing to play if you are."

Jeremey gazed hard at me then seemed to come to some kind of conclusion because, without warning, he kissed me.

This wasn't how I'd thought my first kiss would be. Not that I had given it much thought, mind you. Jeremey pulled me closer, and I melted into him. The sound of people and the thought of where we were seemed to disappear as we stood there and explored this new part of our relationship. The butterflies I thought I had lost came back, and they brought friends. But that delightful feeling of glee to be in Jeremy's arms didn't last long.

Some guy whistled and yelled for us to get a room. Both of our faces turned a warm shade of red, and I couldn't meet Jeremy's eyes.

"Uh." Jeremy coughed and cleared his throat just as flustered as I was. "There's a pair of boots and spare clothes in my truck, if you still want to play with us, that is." Jeremy seemed to be looking everywhere but at me. His face had cooled, but his ears still seemed a little more red than normal. I couldn't help the smile that stretched over my face.

"I'd loved to play."

Muttering under his breath, Jeremy ran a hand through his hair, making it stand every which way. "I'm going to get you some shoes, and uh, yeah." Without saying anything else, he headed to the parking lot, rummaging through his pocket for keys.

It didn't take long to get the clothes and standing in the women's locker room with my brown boots, I geared up with one of the face masks and other protective pads the ballpark loaned me. Putting my bag the locker, I thought again and pulled out my cell.

Tapping in Kylie's name, I typed out a text, deleted it, and typed out a new one. I deleted that one too. In the end, I just sent her the one text that everyone loved to get.

You were right.

I tossed the phone in the locker, slammed the door, and locked it. Taking a fortifying breath, I walked out the door and into something new and a little scary. I marched into the ring and saw all the obstacles and felt a little bit of apprehension.

I spotted Jeremy, and some of that apprehension melted away and was replaced with the feeling of all things fluffy. Whatever happened in the ring tonight, if we won or not, I had one of my best friends by my side again. Not just in this ring but outside of it too. No, things weren't totally fixed yet, but we'd work on it and our relationship. This new thing we both were going to try would be better for it.

Jeremy turned and gave me big grin. Smiling back, I lowered my mask, and I felt more self-assured and confident, knowing I had him with me.

Watching the clock count-down, I hurried and got into my place. I heard the last few beeps as the numbers became single digits and couldn't help the smile that spread across my face. With one last beep, a horn sounded, and the paintballs started flying.

I started the night in a limo going to a dance with the one guy in school everyone wanted on their arm and feeling miserable. But as I crouched behind a metal drum taking fire, I couldn't be happier. And yeah, maybe taking cover behind a metal drum wasn't the best place for a life lesson to come to mind. But was there ever not a good place to learn everything you thought you wanted in life was stupid?

Offering covering fire for a teammate, I waited my turn as we moved up the line and took out more of the opposing team. I carefully took aim and sent off a shot taking out the last guy seconds before the buzzer sounded the end of the first match.

Taking my mask off, I tossed it in the air like the others celebrating our win. The guys slapped my back and congratulated me on the fine shooting. Jeremy came up and pulled me over for a kiss.

"You did amazing, we're going on to the second match after a short break, so let's get some water, huh?" Stunned at his show of affection, I wasn't sure what to say. Holding both our safety masks, Jeremy grabbed my hand and tugged me out of the paint pit with the rest of the team.

Feeling giddy at our first win, I squeezed Jeremy's hand, and those darn butterflies came back with friends when Jeremey pulled me close and swung an arm over my shoulders.

No, this wasn't where most girls would want to be on dance night, but this was where I wanted to be, next to my best friend.

Chapter 31
Kylie.

———

Sitting in the corner booth, I watched the guys re-live the best parts of the night. Paisley sat, covered in paint with Jeremy and his friends, and eating a huge burger. Jeremy had a stupid grin with an arm around Paisley, letting everyone know who she was there with. I honestly couldn't be happier for the two of them. It was about time they got together; it was getting a little ridiculous this point.

I folded my last bird and wrote down the number. Nine hundred and ninety-nine. Putting it in a bag, I zipped it and slurped down the last of my shake and sent a text off for a taxi. "Hey guys, it's been fun, but I'm heading home." Jeremy stole one of Paisley's fries and stuffed it in his mouth, so she took a cherry from his shake and ate it with a smile. Gosh, they were sickeningly cute.

"If you wait, I'll drop you off." Jeremy went for his wallet, but I didn't want to intrude on their first night as a couple and become the third wheel, so I waved him off.

"Haven't you heard, three is a crowd, see ya later. And you missy, owe me a vid chat." Wiggling my eyebrows, I saw both their faces redden, and I smiled at their guilty looks. Flipping my freshly dyed hair over a shoulder, I waved goodbye and headed for the exit.

Getting in the taxi, I took one last look inside. Paisley leaned over and kissed Jeremy on the cheek, and he hugged her close with a goofy grin.

Shutting the door, I told the driver my address and hugged my bag clos-er, trying to hold it all together. Just one more bird to make. If this mag-ic thing worked for Paisley, maybe it will work for me too.

Chapter 32

Was it like how you thought it would be?

The day after the dance, you could clearly see who had drank too much and who hadn't overindulged in the night's fun. A few people didn't even show up at school, and I couldn't help an eye roll at that. I shoved some books in my locker and felt a hand on my shoulder. Smiling, I turned and faced Garrett. Bloodshot eyes and dark rings didn't look good on him.

"Hey." Lame, but what was I going to say to the guy I left standing in the middle of the dance floor alone?

"So, you and that Jeremy guy, huh?" I must have looked perplexed because he just snorted and ran a hand through his hair. "Word traveled fast when people learned I'd been dumped at the dance." Wincing at his tone, I felt bad for how I had dealt with things, but all the questions I'd asked him last night and the way he answered them ran through my head. Mentally shaking my head to clear those thoughts, Emily walked by and waved to me. I waved back with a smile then turned to face Garrett.

"I'm sorry, I really am, but Jeremy..." I huffed out a breath and tried to think of a way to put it without hurting him. "He is my friend. And I think I've loved him a long time. I just didn't fully know it until I almost lost him." I hugged my books tight and willed him to understand. Because this had nothing to do with who he was and everything to do with who Jeremy was.

"Ready to go, Pays?" Jeremy waited a few feet away, shifting from foot to foot looking nervous. I smiled and held up a hand indicating I need a minute more.

"I never had a chance, did I?" I met Garrett's eyes, and all I saw a forlorn look of rejection.

"I'm sorry." An ache started deep, knowing I was hurting him. There was nothing I could say that would heal that hurt or make this better. "Here, you should have this back." I handed him the little heart-shaped necklace and apologized again. He took the gold chain but didn't say anything about it. He just stared at the thing. Feeling the stares of people now, I apologized again because I had nothing better to say and then walked away.

I thought I heard him say, "So am I," but I didn't turn back to ask. I just kept walking. I knew looking back would make it hurt all the more. Jeremy took my hand, and we headed for his truck.

"What was that about?" Jeremy's voice broke into my thoughts as we walked to the doors weaving through all the others, trying to make their way out of school and to whatever they had planned.

"Nothing." I didn't feel up to telling him about the whole thing. I mean, who would believe me? I made a wish on a magical flower. Thinking back, I didn't even believe it myself sometimes.

Jeremey held the door open, and I walked outside. The sun was pleasantly warm on my skin, but not as nice as the feeling of when Jeremy pulled me closer and wrapped an arm around my shoulders.

"Didn't look like..." Jeremey stopped mid-sentence and pulled me to a stop alongside him. "What's with all the flowers. Isn't it too late in the fall for new things to grow?" The whole schoolyard was covered in white daisy's, hundreds of the flowers waved in the breeze.

"Do I look like a flower expert?" I took back whatever I had just thought about that flower wish not being real. Whether people wanted to believe it or not, magic was real. And it helped me see what I had right in front of my own face.

"Nah, you look like my girlfriend." Jeremey bent down and plucked a flower then tucked it behind my ear. Feeling bubbling happiness at his admission, I threaded my fingers through his, and we walked to his truck.

I didn't know where my life was going, and I may not get into the library program I wanted, or Mandy could try to make these last years of school hard on me. But I knew with Jeremy by my side; I could take on anything this world had to throw at me.

Coming soon...

1k Wish is the next book in the series and features Kylie and her paper cranes.

1k Wish

I snuck into his room when he didn't answer my soft knock and crept to the bookcase. The last thing I wanted to do was wake him now that he was resting. I knew where all the squeaky floorboards were and passed them with ease. It wasn't late in the evening yet, but I knew if he was resting, I'd have to wait till tomorrow to show him.

Slowly, I slid the book back into its place with the rest of his collection and smiled to myself. Mission accomplished. "What are you up to, Nieta?" My grandfather's voice was soft and raspy in the gloomy evening shadows.

"Just putting one of your books back. I didn't mean to wake you, Abuelo." I sat in the chair by his bed. The fluff had long ago been flattened from long hours of sitting and waiting.

"Did you have a nice night?" His question was accompanied by a wet cough, and I rushed to get him something to help ease the discomfort.

Sitting him up, I got a glass of water and some of his meds. After he was settled, I propped my feet up on his bed and made myself comfortable. "Yes, grandpa, I had a good night. I just wanted to return your book and show you; I finally did them." Opening both hands to show him my last paper bird. Over the last few weeks, I'd been making them and had finally made one thousand of the little things.

This one was a palest pink and had a little black number on it. I handed it to my grandfather and let him exam it. "What do you think, Abuelo?" I dropped my feet and rocked closer to the bed, not wanting to miss a thing he said.

"Ah, very nice folds, dear, my wife use to make these. See that book over there," He pointed to the book I just returned, and my inside caved in. "Grab it for me, won't you, dear?" I'd just got it back from Paisley's. Thankfully, she hadn't noticed it was gone, being so engrossed with Jeremy to notice I took it back the other night.

Handing it over, I watched him flip the worn pages until he landed on the one with the birds. "Now, my wife liked birds, cranes, especially, see here?" I dutifully looked at the page and saw the illustration of a crane. "If you make one thousand cranes in a year, you will be granted one wish." I nodded and made all the right sounds in all the right places. "Some wish for wealth or other silly things. But you can also wish for health. See here?" He flipped to a new page and sure enough, was a list of things the crane wish was good for. Health was one of them.

I listened and nodded here and there, but it didn't take long for him to talk himself out. I took the book and put it back where it belonged. I placed my little bird on the nightstand and backed out of the room, but I missed a board and made a sound.

My grandfather woke and looked at me then over to the nightstand. "Ah, my wife used to make these. She loved birds, especially cranes." He picked up the little bird and smiled, my heart ached, and I fought back tears as he went through the whole thing again. But what really did me in was when he asked who I was and if I had seen his granddaughter by chance.

With everything I had inside, I hoped the legend of the thousand cranes was true. If the magic worked for Paisley, shouldn't work for me too?

Don't miss out!

Visit the website below and you can sign up to receive emails whenever Beth Lauzier publishes a new book. There's no charge and no obligation.

https://books2read.com/r/B-A-RPAL-SLGGB

BOOKS 2 READ

Connecting independent readers to independent writers.

Did you love *He Loves Me*? Then you should read *Purgatory* by Beth Lauzier!

Three tips for escaping an insane asylum.

1. Avoid the Shadow people. Their a little on the crazy side and prone to maniacal laughter.

2. Run in a zig zag formation and remember to breathe from your diagram.

3. But most importantly, avoid the murderous ghost girl.

When a hidden key leads Ripley and her new friend Scott into a different world, they soon learn some doors should stay closed. Now they have to find their way back home all while avoiding Shadow beasts and a murderous ghost girl who just wants them stay forever.

Purgatory is the first in Beth Lauzier's Nether series. Mysterious, thrilling, and just a touch of murderous ghosts. Strap in and keep the lights on. The door just got unlocked.

Read more at https://www.seriouslyawesomebooks.com.

Also by Beth Lauzier

I Wish Series
He Loves Me

Watch for more at https://www.seriouslyawesomebooks.com.

About the Author

Beth Lauzier is an author of YA fantasy, He Loves Me is the first in the I Wish series of magic-realism. When not writing or reading, you might find her trying to convince the local bird population to rise up and do her bidding. A resident of Longview Texas, Beth Lauzier lives with her family and generally avoids the outside world because books are better and it's too people-y out there.

Read more at https://www.seriouslyawesomebooks.com.